"Love has nothing to do with what is between us."

Her knuckles showed white as she tightened her grip on her glass. "There is nothing between us."

"Look at me and tell me that—show me the courage of your conviction," Rafael derided.

Georgie felt as though she was being torn apart.

"I said...look at me." Rafael scanned her face with scorchingly angry dark eyes. "Do you think I enjoy wanting you? But this time I will not walk away. Why should I? You owe me...."

LYNNE GRAHAM was born in Northern Ireland and has been a keen reader of romance since her teens. She is happily married, with an understanding husband who has learned to cook since she started to write! Her three children, two of whom are adopted, keep her on her toes. She also has a very large wolfhound, who knocks over everything with her tail, and an even more adored mongrel, who rules everybody. When time allows, Lynne is a keen gardener and loves experimenting with Italian cookery.

Books by Lynne Graham

HARLEQUIN PRESENTS

1551—TEMPESTUOUS REUNION
1696—A VENGEFUL PASSION
1712—ANGEL OF DARKNESS
1740—INDECENT DECEPTION
1758—BOND OF HATRED
1779—THE UNFAITHFUL WIFE

LYNNE GRAHAM
Crime of Passion

Harlequin Books

TORONTO • NEW YORK • LONDON
AMSTERDAM • PARIS • SYDNEY • HAMBURG
STOCKHOLM • ATHENS • TOKYO • MILAN
MADRID • WARSAW • BUDAPEST • AUCKLAND

ISBN 0-373-11792-2

CRIME OF PASSION

First North American Publication 1996.

Copyright © 1995 by Lynne Graham.

CHAPTER ONE

THE Bolivian policeman growled across the table. '*Es usted inglesa? Donde se aloja usted?*'

The small room was unbelievably hot and airless. Georgie shot her interrogator a glittering glance from furious violet eyes and threw back her head, a torrent of tousled multi-coloured curls every shade from gold to copper to Titian red dancing round her pale triangular face. 'I do not speak Spanish!' she said for the twentieth time.

He thumped the table with a clenched fist. '*Como?*' he demanded in frustration.

Her teeth gritted, the naturally sultry line of her mouth flattening. Suddenly something just exploded inside her. 'I've been robbed and I've been attacked and I'm not going to just sit here while you shout at me!' she burst out, her strained voice threatening to crack right down the middle.

Plunging upright, the man strode over to the door and threw it wide. Georgie gaped in disbelief as her attacker was ushered in. All the fear she had striven to hide behind her defiant front flooded back, images of rape and violence taking over. She flew up out of her chair and stumbled backwards into the corner, one trembling hand attempting to hitch up the torn T-shirt which threatened to expose the bare slope of her breasts.

Her assailant, a heavily built young man, glowered accusingly and self-righteously across the room at her and burst into vituperative Spanish.

5

Georgie blinked bemusedly. Her own blank sense of incomprehension was the most terrifying aspect of all. Why did the creep who had mauled her in his truck behave as though he was the one entitled to make a complaint to the police? In fact, the lunatic, apparently ignorant of the fact that the attempted sexual assault was a crime, had actually dragged *her* into the tiny, dilapidated police station!

In exaggerated dumb-show, the policeman indicated the bloody tracks of Georgie's nails down one side of the younger man's unshaven face.

Dear heaven, was a woman not allowed to defend herself when she was assaulted in Bolivia? Without warning, the artificial strength of outrage began to fail Georgie. Her independent spirit quailed and, for the first time in her life, she longed for family back-up.

But her father and stepmother were enjoying a three-week cruise of the Greek islands in celebration of their twentieth wedding-anniversary and her stepbrother, Steve, was in central Africa reporting on some civil war that had recently blown up. Her family didn't even know where she was. Georgie had impulsively splurged her late grandmother's legacy on her flight to Bolivia. A once in a lifetime holiday, she had promised herself.

Just thirty-six hours ago she had landed at La Paz, cheerfully anticipating her coming reunion with her friend, María Cristina Reveron. How many times had María Cristina pleaded with her to come and stay? It had undoubtedly never occurred to her friend, an heiress from the day of her birth, that simple lack of money might lie behind Georgie's well-worn excuses. In the same way, it had not occurred to Georgie that María Cristina and her husband, Antonio, might not be in residence when she finally arrived!

The Reveron villa had been closed up, guarded by a security man with two vicious dogs. He had not had a word of English. Refusing to surrender to panic, Georgie had checked into the cheapest hotel she could find and had decided to do a little exploring on her own while she waited for the Reverons to return to La Paz. Since María Cristina was eight months pregnant, Georgie was convinced that her friend could only be away for the weekend at most.

'A little exploring,' she reflected now, on the edge of hysteria as she studied the two angrily gesticulating men several feet away. Panic was threatening her. She was more than out of her depth, she was drowning. Intelligence told her that it was time to play the one card she had refused to play when she found the Reveron villa inconveniently and dismayingly empty of welcoming hosts. The wild card, the one move that she had never dreamt she would ever be forced to make.

She could have phoned Rafael to ask him where his sister was... but her every skin-cell had cringed from the idea of contacting *him*, asking *him* for his assistance. Stupid pride, she saw now, hardly the behaviour of a responsible adult. Four years was a long time. So he had dumped her. So he had hurt and misjudged her. So he had humiliated her. Well, join the real world, Georgie, she taunted herself, with the thickness of tears convulsing her throat, you are not the only woman ever to suffer that way!

Approaching the table, where a notepad and pen lay, Georgie drew in a deep sustaining breath. But suppose they had never heard of Rafael? Suppose he wasn't the big wheel her friend had always led her to believe? And, even if both those fears proved unfounded, just how likely was it that Rafael Cristóbal Rodriguez Berganza would flex a single aristocratic finger to come to her aid?

With an unsteady hand, Georgie carefully block-printed Rafael Rodriguez Berganza across the pad and then pressed it across the table. It hurt to do it—oh, yes, it hurt to write that name.

A furrow appeared between the policeman's brows. With an air of questioning confusion, he looked up and across at her. He repeated the name out loud with more than a touch of reverence. *'No entiendo,'* he said, frowning his lack of understanding.

'Friend! Good friend!' Georgie tapped the pad with feverish desperation and then crossed her arms defensively over her breasts. 'Very good friend,' she lied, forcing a bright and hopefully confident smile, while inside herself she curled up and died with mortification.

The policeman looked frankly incredulous, and then he vented a slightly nervous laugh. He pointed to her and then he tapped his own head and shook it. He cut right across the language barrier. You're nuts, the gesture said.

'I am telling the truth!' Georgie protested frantically. 'I've known Rafael for years. Rafael and I...we're like this!' She clutched her hands together, striving to look sincere and meaningful.

The policeman flushed and studied his shoes, as though she had embarrassed him. Then, abruptly, as the youthful truck-driver exploded back into speech again, the policeman thrust him unceremoniously out of the room and slammed the door on him.

'I want you to telephone Rafael!' Feeling idiotic, but now convinced that she was actually getting somewhere, Georgie mimicked dialling a number and lifting a phone while he watched her.

With a sigh, the policeman moved forward. He clamped a hand round her narrow wrist, prodded her out into the corridor and from there at speed down into the dirty barred cell at the foot. He had turned the key and pocketed it before Georgie even knew what was happening to her.

'Let me out of here!' she shrieked incredulously.

He disappeared out of view. A door closed, sealing her into silence. Georgie stood there, both hands gripping the rusting bars. She was shaking like a leaf. Well, so much for the influence of the Berganza name! A gush of hot burning tears suddenly stung her eyes. She stumbled down on to the edge of the narrow, creaking bed, with its threadbare blanket covering, and buried her aching head in her hands.

About an hour later an ancient woman clad in black appeared, to thrust a plate through a slot in the bars. Georgie hadn't eaten since breakfast but her stomach totally rebelled against the threat of food. The chipped cup of black coffee was more welcome. She hadn't realised how thirsty she was.

After a while she lay down, fighting back the tears. Sooner or later, they would get an interpreter. This whole stupid mess would be cleared up. She did not need Rafael to get her out of trouble. But she was a walking disaster, she decided furiously. Her first solo trip abroad, she had boobed with spectacular effect. Why? She was impulsive, always had been, probably always would be. This was not the first time impetuosity had landed Georgie in trouble... but it was absolutely going to be the last, she swore.

Male voices were talking in Spanish when Georgie wakened. Disorientated, she sat up, hair tumbling in wild disarray round her. The heat was back. The new day pierced a shard of sunlight through the tiny barred window high up the wall. Sleepy violet eyes focused on the two male figures beyond the bars.

One was the policeman, the other was... Her heartbeat went skidding into frantic acceleration. 'Rafael!' she gasped, positively sick with relief in that first flaring instant of recognition.

In the act of offering the policeman a cigar, Rafael
flicked her a stabbing glance from deep-set dark eyes,
treacherous as black ice, and murmured lazily in aside,
'Pull your skirt down and cover yourself...you look
like a whore.'

Without missing a beat in his apparently chummy chat
with the policeman, Rafael presented her with his hard-
edged golden profile again. Georgie's mouth had
dropped inelegantly wide, a tide of burning colour as-
sailing her fair skin. With clumsy hands she scrabbled
rather pointlessly to pull down her denim skirt, already
no more than a modest two inches above the knee. She
fumbled with the sagging T-shirt, angry violet eyes
flashing.

'Don't you dare speak to me like that,' she hissed.

Both male heads spun back.

'If you don't shut up, I walk,' Rafael spelt out, without
an ounce of compassion.

Georgie believed him. That was the terrifying truth.
Just give him the excuse and he would leave her here to
rot—it was etched in the icy impassivity of his slashing
gaze, the unhidden distaste twisting his beautifully
shaped mouth. He had worn that same look four years
ago in London...and then it had almost killed her.

Her throat closed over. Suddenly it hurt to breathe.
She fought back the memories and doggedly lifted her
chin again, refusing with all the fire of her temperament
to be cowed or embarrassed. But Georgie could still wake
up in a cold sweat at night just reliving the humiliation
of their final meeting. She hated Rafael like poison for
the way he had treated her. It was a tribute to the strength
of her fondness for his sister that their friendship had
survived that devastating experience.

As the two men continued to talk, ignoring her with
supreme indifference, Georgie studied Rafael. Against
this shabby setting he looked incongruous, exotically

alien in a fabulously well-cut grey suit, every fibre of which shrieked expense. The rich fabric draped powerful shoulders, accentuated narrow hips and lithe long legs. Her nails clenched convulsively into the hem of her far from revealing skirt. Maybe he thought she looked like a tart because he was so bitterly prejudiced against her.

His photograph had been splashed all over the cover of *Time* magazine the previous summer. Berganza, the Bolivian billionaire, enemy of the corrupt, defender of the weak. Berganza, the great philanthropist, directly descended in an unbroken line from a blue-blooded Castilian nobleman, who had arrived in Bolivia in the sixteenth century. The journalist had lovingly dwelt on his long line of illustrious ancestors.

Georgie had been curious enough to devour the photographs first. He was very tall, but he dominated not by size but by the sheer force of his physical presence. A staggeringly handsome male animal, he was possessed of a devastating and undeniable charisma. His magnificent bone-structure would still turn female heads thirty years from now.

She searched his golden features, helplessly marking the stunning symmetry of each, the wide forehead, the thin arrogant nose and the savagely high cheekbones. She wished she could exorcise him the way she had burned that magazine, in a ceremonial outpouring of self-loathing and hatred. Her voluptuous mouth thinned with the stress of her emotions.

A split-second later, it fell wide again as she watched the 'enemy of the corrupt' smoothly press a handful of notes extracted from his wallet into the grateful policeman's hands. He was bribing him. In spite of the fact that Georgie had always refused to believe in the reality of Rafael Rodriguez Berganza, the saint of the Latin-American media, she was absolutely shattered by the sight of those notes changing hands.

Her cell door swung open. Rafael stepped in. His nostrils flaring as he cast a fastidious glance round the cell, he swept the blanket off the makeshift bed and draped it round her stiff shoulders. 'I almost didn't come,' he admitted without remorse, his fluid, unbearably sexy accent nipping down her taut spinal cord, increasing her tension.

'Then I won't bother saying thanks for springing me,' Georgie stabbed back, infuriated by the concealing blanket he appeared to find necessary and provoked by the unhappy fact that she had to throw her head back just to see him, her height less than his by more than a foot. But beneath both superficial responses lurked a boiling pool of bitter resentment and remembered pain which she was determined to conceal.

'Were it not for my sister, I would have left you here,' Rafael imparted with harsh emphasis. 'It would have been a character-building experience from which you would have gained immense benefit.'

'You hateful bastard!' Georgie finally lost control. Having been subjected to the most frightening experience of her life, his inhuman lack of sympathy was the last straw. 'I've been robbed, assaulted and imprisoned!'

'And you are very close now to being beaten as well, *es verdad*?' Rafael slotted in, his low-pitched voice cracking like a whiplash. 'For if I will not tolerate a man offering me such disrespect, how do I tolerate it from a mere woman?'

Hot-cheeked and furious, Georgie literally stalked out of the cell. A mere woman? How could she ever have imagined herself in love with Rafael Rodriguez Berganza? Then, it hadn't been love, she told herself fiercely. It had been pure, unvarnished lust, masquerading as a bad teenage crush. But at nineteen she had been too mealy-mouthed to admit that reality.

He planted a hand to her narrow back and pushed her down the corridor, and she was momentarily too shaken by the raw depth of naked rage she had ignited in those dark eyes to object. What the blazes did he have to be so angry about? OK, so it had no doubt been inconvenient for him to come and fish her out of a cell at eight in the morning, but dire straits demanded desperate measures and surely even a self-centred swine like him could acknowledge that?

Outside, the sunlight was blinding, but she was disorientated by the crowd of heaving bodies surrounding the two Range Rovers awaiting them outside. With a slight hiss of irritation, Rafael suddenly planted two hands round her waist, swept her off the ground and thrust her into the passenger seat in the front one. Then he turned back to his ecstatic audience.

All the men had their hats off. Some of the women were crying. Kids were pressing round his knees, clutching at him. And then the crowd parted and the policeman reappeared, with an elderly priest by his side. The priest was grinning all over his face, reaching for Rafael's hands, clearly calling down blessings on his head.

What it was to be a hero! It made her stomach heave. Georgie looked away, only to stiffen in dismay as she noticed the squirming sack on the driver's seat. What the blue blazes was in the sack? She shrank up against the door.

Frozen into stillness, Georgie watched the sack wobble and shiver. There was something alive in it, unless she was very much mistaken... With an ear-splitting shriek of alarm, Georgie catapulted herself head-first out of the car. She came down on the hard dusty ground with enough force to knock the breath from her lungs.

'Not happy unless you're the centre of male attention, are you?' Rafael breathed unpleasantly, bending over her as she scrambled up on to her knees. Two of his security men had climbed out of the vehicle behind to see what was happening.

Red as a beetroot but outraged, Georgie gasped, 'There's a snake in that sack!'

'So?' Rafael enquired drily. 'It's a local delicacy.'

He dumped her back in the seat she had left in such haste, the blanket firmly wrapped round her quivering limbs. Perspiring with fright, impervious to the amusement surrounding her, Georgie watched the policeman smilingly tie the sack more securely shut and deposit it back in the car.

'Please take it away, Rafael,' she mumbled sickly, leaning out of the window. '*Please!*'

A lean brown hand reached for the offending article and removed it, putting it in the back seat.

'Thank you,' she whispered as he swung into the driver's seat. A stray shaft of sunlight gleamed over the blue-black luxuriance of his silky hair. Like a reformed kleptomaniac in an untended store of goodies, Georgie clasped her hands, removed her eyes from temptation and hated herself. Why did memory have to be so *physical*? She shifted on the seat, bitterly ashamed that she could still remember just how silky his hair felt.

'So tell me, how—in your view—did you land yourself in a cell less than twenty-four hours after your arrival in my country?' he invited curtly, making it clear that whatever was on his mind, it was certainly not on a similar plane to hers.

'Yesterday, I decided to go and see the Zongo Valley ice-caves——'

'Dressed as you are now?' Rafael cut in incredulously. 'In a mini skirt and high heels?'

'I——' A mini skirt? He regarded a glimpse of her knees as provocative?

'The climb to the caves takes almost two hours even for an experienced hill-walker!'

Georgie's teeth clenched. 'Look, I simply saw this poster in the hotel. I didn't know you had to be an athlete to get up there!'

'When did reality dawn?'

'When I got out of the taxi and saw a trio of brawny, booted, bearded types swarming up the hill,' she admitted in a frozen voice, empty of amusement. 'So I thought I'd walk back and see the lake instead, and I turned back to tell the taxi-driver that I wouldn't be long and he'd gone...with my handbag!'

'Jorge suspected something of that nature.'

'Who is Jorge?'

'The village policeman,' Rafael said drily.

'My bag was stolen. The driver just took off with it on the back seat!'

'It may have been an oversight on his part. Had you asked him to wait?'

Georgie stiffened. 'Well, I thought he understood——'

'Do you know the registration of the taxi?' Rafael surveyed her with an offensive lack of expectation.

Angrily she shook her head.

'Your bag may yet reappear,' Rafael asserted. 'If your bag is not handed in, then you may say that it has been stolen, not before. You were stupendously careless!'

'Lecture over yet?' she demanded shortly.

'When you found yourself stranded, what did you do?'

'By the time I realised he wasn't coming back, the place was deserted, so I started walking and then I...' She hesitated. 'Then I hitched a lift. You wouldn't believe how pleasant and unthreatening the driver was when I got into his truck——'

'I believe you. I should imagine he came to a wheel-screeching halt,' Rafael murmured with withering sarcasm. 'Then what?'

Georgie lifted her chin. 'He offered me money and while I was pushing it away he lunged at me. I thought I was going to be raped!'

'I understand you kneed him in the groin and drew blood. One may assume you are reasonably capable of self-defence. He thought you were a prostitute——'

'A what?' she exploded.

'Why do you think he offered you money? Female tourists do not travel alone in Bolivia, nor do they hitch alone.' Grim dark eyes flicked a glance at her outraged face before returning to the road.

'Have you any idea how scared I was when he drove off and wouldn't let me out of his truck?'

'He was determined to report you for what he saw as an attempt to rip him off. But he was happy to drop the charge once he realised that his neighbours would laugh heartily at him for being attacked by a woman half his size!'

Georgie was enraged by his attitude. The message was: you asked for it.

'You had a very narrow escape. He might have beaten you up to avenge the slur upon his manhood. This country has been dominated by the cult of *machismo* for four centuries,' Rafael drawled in a murderously polite tone. 'It will take more than a handful of tourists to change that but, happily, the great majority of travellers are infinitely more careful of their own safety than you have been.'

'So I asked for what I got . . . in *your* view!' she flared.

'An attempted kiss, a hand on your knee—he swore that was all. He said you went crazy and I believe him. It'll be weeks before he can show his face without his neighbours sniggering.' Rafael actually sounded sympathetic towards the truck-driver.

Silence stretched endlessly. He made no attempt to break it. The four-wheel-drive lurched and bounced over the appalling road surface with the vehicle behind following at a discreet distance. Briefly, Rafael stopped the car and sprang out. Incredulously she watched him open the sack to release the snake. Wow, environmentally friendly man, and sensitive enough not to offend the villagers by refusing the unwanted gift. It crossed her mind bitterly that the snake was getting more attention than she was.

Then, that was hardly a surprise. Four years ago, Rafael had made it brutally clear that she failed his standards in every way possible. Her morals, her behaviour—her sexually provocative behaviour, she recalled angrily—had all been comprehensively shredded by that cruel, whiplash tongue. But what still hurt the most, she was honest enough to admit, was that she hadn't had the wit to take it on the chin and walk away with dignity. Like a fool, she had attempted to prove her innocence.

'He's from a different world,' her stepbrother Steve had derided once. 'And he belongs to a culture you don't even begin to understand. Don't be fooled by the fact that he speaks English as well as we do. Rafael's a very traditional Latin-American male and the women in his life fall into two categories. Angels and whores. The females in his family—they're the angels. The females who share his bed—they're the whores. When he marries, he'll select an angel straight out of a convent and she'll be as well-born and rich as he is. So where are you planning to fit in?'

And ultimately Steve had been proved right, that dreadful evening when her short-lived relationship with Rafael had been blown apart at the seams. Rafael *had* treated her like a whore. Scorched by that memory,

Georgie sank back to the present and cast aside the swel-
tering blanket in a gesture of rebellion. She stretched out
her lithe, wonderfully shapely legs and crossed them.
She didn't give two hoots for *his* opinion, did she? She
wasn't a stupid, besotted little teenager any more, was
she?

'Where are you staying in La Paz?' he asked after a
perceptible pause, firing the engine again.

She told him. That was the end of the conversation,
but the atmosphere was so thick all of a sudden that
she could taste it. It tasted like oil waiting for a flame—
explosive. She tilted her head back, a helplessly feminine
smile of satisfaction curving her lips as she noticed the
tense grip of his lean hands on the wheel. So, in spite
of all the insults, Rafael was still not impervious to her
on the most basic level of all. A little voice in the back
of her mind demanded to know what she was doing,
why she was behaving in this utterly uncharacteristic way.
She suppressed it.

She was surprised when he sprang out of the car and
silently accompanied her into her shabby hotel, but she
chose not to comment. Why lower herself to talk to him?
She strolled ahead of him, every tiny swing of her hips
an art-form. Presumably he was intending to take her
straight to his sister. María Cristina was probably home
again by now. But how on earth was Georgie to settle
her hotel bill? Her missing handbag had contained not
only her passport, but all her money as well.

Her room looked as though a bomb had hit it. Yesterday, she had gone out in a rush. Reddening, Georgie
grabbed up her squashy travel-bag and snatched up dis-
carded items of clothing and stuffed them out of sight.
Rafael lounged back against the door, like a bloody great
black storm-cloud, she found herself thinking, suddenly
made nervous and grossly uncomfortable by his presence
in the comparative isolation of the small room.

'You can wait outside while I get changed,' she muttered, because there was no *en suite* bathroom, just a washbasin.

'Don't be ridiculous,' Rafael murmured very drily.

'I am not being ridiculous,' Georgie returned tautly, her colour heightening even more. Dear heaven, surely he wasn't seriously expecting her to strip in front of him?

Intent black eyes collided with violet bemusement. *Whoosh*! It was like grasping a live wire, plunging a finger into a light-socket. Violent shock thundered through Georgie's suddenly taut body. She was electrified, wildly energised, before she strained mental bone and sinew to shut out the rich dark entrapment of his gaze, badly shaken by that terrifying burst of raw excitement.

No...no, it simply couldn't happen to her again. She was immune to all that smouldering Latin-American masculinity now. She had not felt like that, she told herself frantically. She had not felt that stabbing, shooting sensation of almost unbearable physical awareness which had reduced her to such mindless idiocy in the past. That was behind her now, a mortifying teenage crush in which hormones had briefly triumphed over all else.

Rafael bent down fluidly and lifted a silky white pair of very brief panties off the worn carpet and tossed them to her. Already sufficiently on edge, Georgie failed to catch them and ended up scrabbling foolishly on the floor, stuffing the wretched things into her bag with hands that were trembling so badly that they were all fingers and thumbs.

'You wouldn't have given me a knee in the groin,' Rafael murmured very softly.

Crouching over her bag, Georgie slewed wildly confused eyes in his direction, chose to focus safely on his Italian leather shoes.

He moved forward. She froze, the sound of her own breathing loud in her ears.

'You would have knocked me flat with enthusiasm,' Rafael completed thickly.

Bastard, she thought, absolutely shattered by his cruelty. She had believed she was in love, had held nothing back, had often told herself since that she was lucky he had dumped her before she ended up in his bed. But now shame drenched her and she hated him for that. He didn't have to make her sound so *cheap*, did he? In the most essential way of all, she had been innocent, and there had been nothing calculated about her response to him.

'Teenagers aren't very subtle when they have a crush on someone.' Determined not to show that his cracks had got to her, Georgie even managed a sharp little laugh.

'But it wasn't a crush,' Rafael breathed, subjecting her to the full onslaught of deep-set dark eyes that disturbingly lingered and somehow held her evasive gaze steady. 'You were violently in love with me.'

Georgie very nearly choked. The bag in her hand dropped unnoticed as her fingers lost their grip. Abruptly, she turned away, sick inside. What kind of sadist was he? Did it give him some sort of perverse kick to throw that in her teeth? It had not been love, it had *never* been love—she had told herself that ever since.

'And the vibrations are still there...I feel them,' Rafael delivered in a purring undertone that still sliced through the throbbing silence.

'I feel nothing...nothing!' Georgie threw back tremulously over her shoulder, wildy disconcerted by the direction of the dialogue, it having been the last subject she would have believed him likely to refer to. She had thought herself safe from any reference to the past, had been grimly aware of his aloof detachment. Now the tables were turned with a vengeance.

Rafael reached out a strong hand and spun her back to face him. 'Why pretend? We're both adults now, and I know that you take your pleasure where and when you find it... and with any man who attracts you.'

Oxygen rasped in her throat and she trembled under the onslaught of that character assassination, fighting off the memories threatening to assail her. 'How dare you?'

Insolent dark eyes mocked her ferocious tension and her sudden pronounced pallor. He lifted his other hand calmly and ran a forefinger along the full curve of her taut lower lip. 'Does it scare you that I know you for what you are? Why should that matter? We don't have to like each other, we don't even have to talk,' he murmured in a deep, dark voice. 'I just want you in that bed under me once... and I really don't care if it *is* sordid, I'll still be the best lover you've ever had.'

The fingertip grazing her lip was sending tiny little shivers through her. Georgie tried and failed to swallow. She couldn't believe what he was saying to her. She just couldn't get her mind round the shock of such a proposal. 'You have to be joking...'

He laughed softly. 'You were always so honest... in this, if nothing else,' he breathed, with a sudden edge of harshness roughening his intonation. 'You want me. I want you. Why should we not make love?'

Georgie shuddered with barely concealed fury, but beneath the fury was a pain she flatly refused to acknowledge. 'Because I *don't* want you! I'm not that desperate!' she spelt out hotly, and jerked free of him, ashamed that her breasts were swollen and full beneath her wispy bra, ashamed that it should actually have taken will-power to step back, and ashamed that for a split-second she had allowed herself to think of that intimacy she had once craved with the man she loved.

Yes, loved—why continue to pretend otherwise when even he knew just how deeply she had been involved? A small sop to pride? 'We're both adults now.' The ultimate humiliation and he just hadn't been able to resist the temptation. She was good enough for a sleazy roll in a grotty hotel room, not good enough for anything else, and even with all that smooth sophistication and experience at his fingertips he hadn't bothered to wrap up that reality.

'I'd like you to leave,' Georgie said with as much dignity as she could muster, and it was not a lot.

'I won't visit you in London. There will be no second chance. You see, I know where you live,' he spelt out with sizzling bite, his dark golden features rigidly cast.

Georgie lived in a tiny attic flat of a terraced house which belonged to her stepbrother, Steve. But the significance of Rafael's reference to that fact quite escaped her. What did where she lived have to do with anything? she wondered briefly, but she was in such turmoil that the oddity of the comment as quickly left her mind again.

She was enraged by the awareness that Rafael had not expected her to refuse that sordid proposition. Rafael had actually expected her to spread herself willingly on the bed. Her narrow shoulders rigid, she turned back to him. 'Just forget where I live——'

'I try to.' Rafael dealt her a chilling look of derision, his nostrils flaring. 'But why else did you come to Bolivia? You knew we would meet again...and that was what you wanted, *es verdad*?'

Georgie was stunned by his arrogance. 'Like hell it was! I want nothing to do with you...absolutely nothing!'

'Prove it,' he taunted, reaching out without warning to drag her up against him with an easy strength that shook her.

'Get your hands off me!' she gasped.

But his mouth crashed down on hers, hard, hungry, hot, forcing her lips apart. And, for Georgie, the world rocked right off its axis, dredging a shocked whimper of sound from deep in her throat. Every physical sense she possessed was violently jolted. His tongue expertly probed the sensitive interior of her mouth, blatantly imitating an infinitely more intimate penetration, and her bones turned to water and she quivered and moaned, electrified by the fierce excitement he awakened. He crushed her slender length to him with bruising hands and she gasped, her thighs trembling, an unbearable ache stirring low in her stomach.

Rafael lifted his dark head slowly. 'Do I take you on that bed or do I take you to the airport?' he prompted silkily, blatant masculine satisfaction in the narrowed gaze scanning her rapt face. 'The choice is yours.'

CHAPTER TWO

'THE *airport*?' Georgie repeated blankly, endeavouring to return to rational thought and finding it unbelievably difficult.

'For your flight home,' Rafael extended, with a slashing and sardonic smile.

'But I'm not going home.' Georgie broke slowly from the loosened circle of his arms, still reeling from the effects of his lovemaking and trying very hard not to show just how shattered she was by the response he had dredged from her. She was in shock. 'I'm going to stay with María Christina.'

'My sister is in California.'

'California?' Georgie parroted after a shattered pause. Incredulously she stared at him. 'What are you talking about?'

'Antonio's mother lives there and María Cristina and Rosa are very close,' Rafael explained smoothly. 'My sister is expecting her first child and, since her own mother is dead, it is natural that she should want Rosa's support at such a time.'

Georgie was in a daze. 'But I received a letter from her less than two weeks ago, inviting me over here. She hoped I'd still be here when she had her baby!'

'She only decided to go to San Francisco last week. She couldn't have been expecting you to come.' Rafael exhibited a magnificent disregard for her natural distress.

'It was a last-minute decision and I got cancellation tickets,' Georgie conceded tautly. 'I tried to phone her the night before the flight but she wasn't in——'

'But you came all the same,' Rafael drawled with an ironic lack of surprise.

'I wanted to surprise her!' Georgie slung back. 'Why didn't you tell me immediately? Obviously you knew I was here to stay with your sister——'

'I had hoped you were not that foolish. I told you to stay away from María Cristina four years ago,' he reminded her with grim emphasis. 'It is a most unsuitable friendship and I made my feelings clear then——'

'Stuff your bloody feelings!' Georgie gasped, suddenly swinging away from him, her voice embarrassingly choked. 'My friendship with María Cristina is none of your business.'

Her bruised eyes were filled with tears. So this was what it felt like to be at the end of her tether. She had really been looking forward to staying with her friend. This disappointment was the last straw. She also knew that, as a recently graduated student teacher, who had yet to find employment, it would be many years before she could hope to repeat such an expensive trip.

It was unlikely that María Cristina would come to London under her own steam. Rafael's sister was very much a home-bird, who had only tolerated her English boarding-school education because it had been her late mother's wish and who had freely admitted that she hadn't the faintest desire to ever leave Bolivia again once her education was completed. Her marriage to a doctor, no more fond of travelling than she was, had set the seal on that insularity.

'Anything which threatens my family is my business.'

'Threatens?' Georgie queried jerkily, fighting for composure. 'And how do I threaten your family?'

'I will not allow you to hurt my sister, and the day that she realises what kind of a woman you really are, she will be hurt.'

'God forgive you...I would never hurt María Cristina!' Georgie gasped painfully, swinging back to him in a rage. 'She'd be a whole lot more hurt if she knew that the brother she idolises is a slimy toe-rag!'

'What did you call me?' Dark eyes had turned incandescent gold, his savagely handsome features freezing into sudden incredulous stillness.

Georgie vented a shaky little laugh. All that bowing and scraping people did in his vicinity did not accustom him to derision. But she knew that she would never forget the depths to which he had sunk in his desire to humiliate her today. 'I think you heard me, and let me assure you that your seduction routine leaves a lot to be desired!' she spelt out, hot with anger and bitterness.

'Seduction was quite unnecessary,' Rafael asserted softly, his beautifully shaped mouth twisting with blatant contempt. 'If I'd kept quiet, I'd be inside you now, and the only sounds in this room would be your moans of pleasure. You'd share a bed with any man who attracted you! I don't pride myself on the idea that there is anything exclusive about your response to me.'

Georgie was trembling violently. Every scrap of colour had drained from her features, leaving her white as snow. Her hand flew up of its own volition but steel-hard fingers snapped round her wrist in mid-air.

'Don't you dare,' Rafael grated down at her in a snarling undertone.

And the violence in the atmosphere was explosive, catching her breath in her dry throat. Raw aggression had flared in his smouldering gaze and instinctively she backed away, massaging her bruised wrist as he freed her, her heartbeat thumping so loudly in her ears that she felt faint and sick, but still she wanted to kill him, still she wanted to punish him for saying those filthy things to her.

'I'm not like that,' she murmured tightly, turning away, despising the little shake that had somehow crept into her voice, betraying her distress. 'And even if I was, it would be a cold day in hell before I let you touch me.'

There was so much more she wanted to say but she didn't trust herself. Once before, she had attempted to reason with Rafael in her own defence. He hadn't listened. He had shot her every plea down in flames, immovably convinced that she had betrayed him in another man's bed. Afterwards she had felt even more soiled and humiliated by his derision. She would never put herself in that position again.

The silence went on forever, reverberating around her in soundless waves.

'Are you able to settle your bill here?'

Four centuries of ice in that chilling enquiry—well, what did she care? Numbly she shook her head.

'I'll take care of it.'

For five minutes, she simply stayed there in the empty room, struggling harder than she had ever had to struggle for control. When she had managed it, she walked down to Reception and found him just moving away from the desk. Without once glancing in his direction, she climbed back into the Range Rover. He would take her to the airport, put her on a flight back home. She really didn't care any more.

The silence smouldered, chipping away at nerves that were already raw and bleeding. 'I presume you can take care of the passport problem,' she muttered, half under her breath, thinking of the bribery he had apparently employed to get her out of her cell.

'What passport problem?' His accented drawl was dangerously quiet.

'Well, obviously it went with everything else in my bag,' she pointed out, surprised that he hadn't grasped that fact yet.

He uttered a raw imprecation in his own language.

'Oh, don't be shy...say it in English!' Georgie suddenly heard herself rake back with a sob in her voice. 'You think I'm a stupid bitch!'

'Georgie...' Fluent though his English was, he couldn't quite handle the two syllables of her name coming so close to each other. He slurred them slightly, his rich dark voice provoking painful memories. 'Don't start crying——'

'I am not crying!' She bit her tongue, tasted blood, blinked back the scorching tide dammed up behind her eyelids.

Soon after that, he stopped the car and got out, leaving her alone for about ten minutes. She waited, enveloped by a giant cloud of unfamiliar depression. It took Rafael to do this to her. He slammed a lid down on her usually bubbly personality. He made her seethingly, horribly angry. And he hurt her. Nothing had changed. She didn't even lift her head when he rejoined her.

'We're here.'

Rafael opened the door. One of his security men already had her bag in one beefy hand.

Rafael extended a black coat.

'What's this?' Georgie had yet to focus on any part of him above the level of his sky-blue silk tie.

'I bought it for you. You cannot walk through the airport with—with your top falling off,' Rafael shared flatly.

She wanted to laugh, because she had managed to forget that she was still wearing yesterday's torn and dirty clothes. But somehow she couldn't laugh. She stuck her arms in the sleeves of the expensive silk-lined raincoat. It was light as a feather but so long it had to look like a nun's habit. Numbly she watched Rafael's fingers do up the buttons. It took him a surprisingly long time, his hands less deft than she had expected.

His double standards were perhaps what she most loathed about Rafael Rodriguez Berganza. He had undoubtedly stripped more women than Casanova. María Cristina had been a gossip while they were at school. Rafael had a notorious reputation for loving and leaving beautiful women. But Georgie would have *known* anyway.

Many very good-looking men missed out on being sexy. But not Rafael. Rafael was a blatantly sexual male animal, flagrantly attuned to the physical. The air around him positively sizzled. So why the heck was this sophisticated, experienced Latin-American lover having so much difficulty buttoning up her coat? Unwarily she collided with glittering golden eyes, and it was like being struck by lightning.

He was so close she could smell a hint of citrusy aftershave, overlying clean, husky male. Her nostrils flared. Her nipples tightened into painful sensitivity, a spiralling ache twisting low in her stomach. Nearby, someone cleared their throat. She tore her gaze from Rafael's and met the looks of visible fascination emanating from his bodyguards, standing several feet away. She realised that she and Rafael had simply been standing there staring at each other. Devastated by her overpowering physical awareness of him, Georgie turned away, her throat closing over.

In silence they entered the airport. Her head felt incredibly light and her lower limbs weak and clumsy. Exhaustion, stress and lack of food, she registered, were finally catching up with her.

Officialdom leapt out of nowhere at them. The crowds parted. Uniformed guards paved every step through the airport, down an eerily empty concourse, their footsteps echoing. There was no sign of other passengers. Clearly she was being put on the flight home either first or last.

As they emerged into the fresh air and crossed the tarmac, she realised incredulously that Rafael intended to see her right on to the plane to be sure she went. It made her feel as though she was being deported in disgrace. And that was when it happened—something that had never happened to Georgie before. As she fought to focus on him and say something smart on parting, her head swam alarmingly. The blackness folded in and she fainted.

'Lie still.' As Rafael made the instruction for the second time and Georgie attempted to defy it, he lost patience and planted a powerful hand to her shoulder, to force her back into the comfortable seat in which she was securely strapped. 'I don't want you to swoon again.'

If he used that word again, she would surely hit him. 'I didn't swoon, I passed out!' she hissed, twisting away from his unwelcome ministrations. 'And will you take that wet flannel out of my face?'

Dense black lashes screened his clear gaze from her view, a curious stillness to his strong, dark face. 'I was trying to help,' he proffered very quietly.

'I don't want your help.' She turned her head away defensively.

You swooned with Rafael and you really hit the jackpot, though, she conceded. The entire aircrew seemed to be hovering with wet flannels, tablets, and glasses of water and brandy. Any minute now the pilot would appear and offer her some fresh air! Dear Lord, she hoped *not!* Her violet eyes widened in disbelief on the clouds swirling past the port-hole across the aisle... they were already airborne!

'What are you doing on this flight?' Georgie demanded, feverishly short of breath. 'We've already taken off!'

Rafael rose up off his knees, smoothed down the knife creases on his superbly tailored trousers and said something to the crew. Everybody went into retreat. He lowered his long, lithe frame fluidly into the seat opposite and fixed hooded dark eyes on her.

'This is my private jet.'

'Your what?' Georgie gaped at him.

'I am taking you home with me. Until your passport can be replaced, you are stuck in Bolivia.'

'But I don't have to be stuck with you!'

Unexpectedly, Rafael sent her a shimmering, sardonic smile. 'A lamb to the slaughter...I don't think.'

'I don't know what the heck you're getting at, but I do know you could have left me in my hotel...or thrown a few backhanders in the right direction the way you did to get me out of my prison cell!' Georgie derided, horrified at the prospect of being forced to accept his grudging hospitality.

He went white beneath his dark skin, his facial muscles freezing. 'How dare you accuse me of sinking to such a level?' he ground out incredulously. 'I have never stooped to bribery in my life!'

Georgie licked at her dry lips. 'I saw you give the policeman the money,' she whispered.

Rafael surveyed her with growing outrage, registering with an air of disbelief that his denial had not been accepted. 'I do not believe that I am hearing this. The policeman, Jorge, took the money straight to the village priest! The roof of the village church has fallen in and my donation will repair it, thereby enhancing Jorge's standing in the community but granting him no personal financial gain,' Rafael spelt out with biting emphasis. 'I wanted to reward him for his efforts on your behalf. Although he did not believe that you were entitled to claim my friendship, and he was afraid of being made to look foolish, he telephoned me. Were it not for his persistence and his conscientious scruples, you would still be in that cell!'

His explanation made greater sense of the villagers' response to him than her own hasty assumption that he had used cash to grease the wheels of justice. She reddened, but she did not apologise.

'The young truck-driver had lied about you but he withdrew his story,' Rafael continued icily. 'You were then free to leave without any further output from me. I did nothing but straighten out a misunderstanding.'

She bent her head, her empty stomach rumbling. 'Do you think you could feed me while you lecture me?'

'Feed you?'

'I haven't eaten since breakfast yesterday.'

'*Por Dios,*' Rafael grated with raw impatience. 'Why did you not say so?'

A microwaved meal arrived at speed. Georgie ate, grateful for any excuse not to have to speak while she attempted to put her thoughts in order. 'I am taking you home with me,' he had said, as if she was a stray dog or cat. 'Home' was the ancestral *estancia* on the vast savannah bounded by the Amazon. And the concept of Rafael taking her back there quite shattered Georgie. Even when she had been María Cristina's best friend at school, Rafael had blocked his sister's every request to bring Georgie out to stay on the *estancia* with them during the holidays.

Memory was taking her back, although she didn't want it to. Georgie had won a fee-assisted place at an exclusive girls' school to study for her A levels. She had met María Cristina in the lower sixth. At half-term, she had invited her friend home for the weekend but, in some embarrassment, the Bolivian girl had explained that her brother, Rafael, who was her guardian, would not allow that unless he had first met Georgie and her parents.

Georgie's father had been amused when he received a phone call from Rafael, requesting permission to take Georgie out for the afternoon in company with his sister.

'Charming but very formal for this day and age,' he had pronounced. 'You'd better mind your "p"s and "q"s there, my girl. I think you're about to be vetted.'

Georgie still remembered coming down the steps in front of the school as the limousine swept up. She had guessed just by the way María Cristina talked that her friend was from a wealthy background, but she had not been prepared for a stretch limousine complete with chauffeur and security men. Then Rafael appeared and Georgie had been so busy looking at him that she had missed the last step and almost fallen flat on her face.

He had reached out and caught her before she fell, laughing softly, dark eyes rich as golden honey sweeping her embarrassed face. 'My sister said you were accident-prone.'

As María Cristina introduced them, his hand had lingered on hers, his narrowed gaze oddly intent until rather abruptly he had stepped back, a slight flush accentuating his hard cheekbones.

He had taken them to the Ritz for afternoon tea. Georgie had been quieter than she had ever been in her life before and painfully shy, a condition equally new to her experience. Right from that first moment of meeting, Rafael had attracted her to a frighteningly strong degree. And Georgie hadn't known how to handle that attraction. It had come out of nowhere and swallowed her alive, draining her of self-will. She had sat there on the edge of her seat, barely able to take her eyes off him, terrified he would notice.

After the Ritz, he had taken them shopping in Harrods. María Cristina had casually spent an absolute fortune on trifles, and when Rafael had bought his sister a gold locket he had insisted on buying one identical for Georgie, smoothly dismissing her protests. Then he had ferried them back to her parents' home where he had been invited to stay to dinner.

Newly conscious of just how rich her friend and her brother were, Georgie had been uncomfortable at first, fearfully watching for any signs of snobbish discomfiture from either of them. Her father was a primary schoolteacher and her stepmother, Jenny, a post-office clerk. Their home was a small, neat semi-detached. Half the neighbourhood had come out to stare at the stretch limousine. But Rafael and María Cristina had made themselves perfectly at home with her family... Steve hadn't been there that first time, Georgie recalled absently.

'Do you want to know the only thing Rafael asked about you?' María Cristina had laughed after her brother had gone, shaking her head in wonderment. 'Is that hair natural?'

For the remainder of her time at school, Georgie had been included in all of her friend's term-time outings with her brother. Gradually she had lost her awe of Rafael, learning to judge her reception by the frequency of that rare and spontaneous smile of his that turned her heart inside out, but also learning to accept that he observed strict boundaries in his behaviour towards her and was prone to cool withdrawal when her impulsive tongue came anywhere near breaching that barrier.

'Rafael likes you,' María Cristina had said once—just one of many desperately gathered little titbits.

'You make him laugh...'

'He thinks you're very intelligent...'

'He wonders why you aren't studyng Spanish...' What an agony of hope that had put her in! But then, it hadn't all been good news.

'He thinks you flirt too much...'

'He said if you wore your skirts any shorter, you'd be arrested...'

'He believes that the two of us will only be adults when we stop telling each other absolutely everything!'

But Georgie had never told María Cristina whose photograph she kept in that locket which she wore constantly. She had been horribly embarrassed the day her friend chose to tease her about that secrecy in front of Rafacl. He had silenced his sister. Dark eyes had intercepted Georgie's anxious gaze and he had smiled lazily, and she had known that he knew perfectly well that it was his photo, taken by her with immensely careful casualness the previous year.

She had met Danny Peters at a sports event a few months before she sat her final exams. They had run into each other several times, quickly forming an easy friendship. Danny had just been ditched by his steady girlfriend and Georgie had supplied a sympathetic ear. When he had asked Georgie to attend his school formal with him, she had agreed, well aware that he merely wanted to save face in front of his friends. It had been a fun night out, nothing more. But María Cristina had gone all giggly about it and had insisted on talking about Danny as Georgie's boyfriend. Had she mentioned Danny to Rafael?

For, one week later, Georgie had come home from visiting her grandmother one afternoon and a scarlet Ferrari had been parked in the driveway. She had raced into the house and frozen on the threshold of the lounge, seeing only Rafael, nothing else but Rafael impinging on her awareness. His very presence in her home without his sister in tow had told Georgie all she needed to know.

'Rafael thought you might like to go for a drive,' her stepmother had mumbled in a dazed voice. 'You should get changed.'

She remembered Steve catching her by the arm before she disappeared into her bedroom. 'He's going to make a bloody fool of you,' he had condemned in a furious undertone. 'But money talks, doesn't it? I can't believe my mother is encouraging him!'

Georgie sank back to the present. With a not quite steady hand, she massaged her stiff neck and strove not to lift her head and look at Rafael. But it was so difficult when she was remembering that glorious afternoon, the sheer joy that he had come, the overwhelming excitement of just being alone with him for the very first time. She had walked on air into that Ferrari.

Before he reversed the car, he had lifted a hand and quite calmly reached for her locket to open it. And then he had smiled lazily, pressed a teasing promise of a kiss against her readily parted lips and dropped a bunch of red roses on her lap. 'If it had been anyone else, I do believe I would have killed you,' he had laughed softly.

He had been outrageously confident of his reception, hadn't even tried to hide the fact. Georgie had had the bewildering feeling that she was being smoothly slotted into a pre-arranged plan, and in a sense that had offended her pride. She might have been head over heels in love with Rafael but she hadn't liked the idea that he knew it too.

He had been entirely complacent about the idea that she had spent eighteen months waiting for him to show an interest in her, that he was indeed her first real boyfriend...if a male of his sophistication could even qualify for such a label. But he had also been careful to tell her that the day she told her sister she was seeing him, their relationship would be at an end. At the time, not telling

María Cristina had really hurt. But later she had been grateful that she had kept quiet.

'She's asking you if you want coffee.'

Georgie's head jerked up, her cheeks warming as she found both the stewardess and Rafael regarding her enquiringly. 'I'd love some,' she mumbled, shaking her head as if to clear it and hurriedly fixing her attention elsewhere.

Rafael added that she liked her coffee with both milk and sugar.

Georgie tensed, childishly tempted to say she now took it black and unsweetened but biting her lip instead. Four years ago, Rafael had chosen her food for her, and had allowed her only the occasional glass of wine, refusing to allow her any other form of alcohol in his company.

'He's a flipping tyrant,' Steve had sneered that final evening, witnessing Rafael's unashamed domination in action. 'I can't believe the way you let him order you around. If you want a drink, I'll get it for you!'

And he had. He had got her several, just daring Rafael to interfere. Georgie did not want to recall where that foolishness had led. Her cup in an unsteady hand, she sipped at her coffee, badly shaken by the uncontrollable force of the memories washing over her.

It had upset Georgie then that her stepbrother and Rafael should barely be able to tolerate each other. Nor had she ever been able to decide who was most at fault—Steve for being a bossy, interfering big brother, who didn't like to see his kid sister being bossed about by anyone else, or Rafael for never once utilising an ounce of his smooth diplomacy in Steve's hot-headed direction.

In those days she had been very proud of Steve's success as a photo-journalist. He was four years her senior, her brother in all but blood ties, and she had relied heavily on Steve's opinions, Steve's advice... And then those ties had been almost completely severed the same night that she had lost Rafael. Truly the worst night of her life, she conceded painfully.

'This is Rurrenabaque,' Rafael informed her as the jet came in to land.

Georgie concentrated on the fantastic views as the land dropped dramatically away below them to spread out into the thickly forested expanse of the Amazon basin. Less than half an hour after landing they were airborne again in a helicopter, from which she saw the very physical evidence of the logging operations in the area. Then the rough tracks forged by man-made machinery petered to a halt, leaving them flying over untouched wilderness, broken only by lonely mountain plateaus and dark winding rivers until the rainforest finally gave way to the vast savannah, cleared centuries earlier for cattle ranching.

'You will want to rest.' Rafael sprang down from the helicopter in her wake and something she caught in his voice made her turn her head.

She met icy dark eyes, read the harsh line of his compressed mouth and the fierce tension in his strong features as he stared fulminatingly back at her. He doesn't want me here. That reality hit her like a bucket of cold water on too-hot skin. Defensively she looked away again, wondering why on earth he had brought her to his home if he felt that strongly and cursing her own weakened, stressed condition earlier.

'At the airport, you let me think you were going to put me on a flight home,' she reminded him accusingly. 'Why didn't you tell me the truth?'

'I was abducting you,' Rafael delivered smoothly. 'Why would I explain my intentions in advance?'

Her bright head spun back, violet eyes wide, her brow furrowed. Then she laughed a little breathlessly. 'I never could tell when you were joking and when you were serious!'

'You will learn.' Unreadable dark eyes glittered intently over her animated face. 'I'm looking forward to teaching you.'

CHAPTER THREE

SUDDENLY cold, even in the sunlight, Georgie stilled. Two dark-skinned men were attending to their luggage. Rafael spoke to them in a language that was definitely not Spanish and then strode forward to greet the older man who was approaching them.

He was Rafael's estate manager, Joaquín Paez. He shook hands with her. 'Señorita Morrison,' he murmured gravely, with an old-world courtesy much in keeping with their gracious surroundings.

The *estancia* was a beautiful white villa, built in the Spanish style. The rambling spacious contours hinted at the alterations made by different generations. Fabulous gardens, lushly planted with shrubs and mature trees, ringed the house, and beyond she could see a whole host of other buildings stretching into the distance. María Cristina had told her that the ranch was a self-contained world of its own, with homes for its workers and their families, a small school, a church and even accommodation for the business conferences which Rafael occasionally held here.

A small, plump woman in a black dress appeared as they reached the elegant veranda at the front of the house. As Rafael addressed her in Spanish, the little woman's smile faltered. She shot a shocked glance at Georgie and then quickly glanced away again to mutter something that just might have been a protest to Rafael.

Georgie hovered, feeling incredibly uncomfortable. Of course they weren't talking about her...why should they be? She was here at the Berganza home on sufferance

until such time as her passport could be replaced. Rafael
had come to her aid when she got herself locked up in
prison purely because she was his sister's friend and
María Cristina would have been deeply shocked had he
done otherwise. In the same way, Rafael's sister would
doubtless also expect her brother to offer hospitality to
Georgie in her own unfortunate absence.

So, Rafael was grimly going through the civilised mo-
tions for the sake of appearances, Georgie told herself.
María Cristina had no idea how her brother and her best
friend felt about each other and, at this late stage, neither
one of them could wish to be forced to make pointless
explanations. Georgie's passport would be replaced
within record time if Rafael had anything to do with
it ... she was convinced of that fact.

'My housekeeper, Teresa, will show you to your room,'
Rafael drawled.

Teresa, whose wide smile had almost split her face on
their arrival, now bore a closer resemblance to a little
stone statue. With a bowed head, the housekeeper moved
a hand, indicating that Georgie should follow her.

Georgie entered the impressive hall and stepped on to
an exquisite Persian rug, spread over a highly polished
wooden floor. Rafael swept off through one of the heavy,
carved doors to the left. A wrought-iron staircase of
fantastically ornate design wound up to the floors above.
Georgie climbed it in Teresa's rigid-backed wake. The
walls were covered with paintings, some of which were
clearly very old. They crossed a huge landing, Georgie's
heels clicking at every step. A door was flung wide with
a faint suggestion of melodrama.

'What a heavenly room,' Georgie whispered helplessly, absorbing a level of opulence which quite took
her breath away. And the décor was so wonderfully
feminine, from the delicate contours of the gleaming antique furniture to the gloriously draped bed awash with

lace. Lemon and blue and white—her favourite colours. Doors led out on to a balcony, adorned with tubs of riotously blooming flowers.

Unselfconscious in her enchantment, Georgie walked past the silent older woman and opened a door that revealed first a fully fitted dressing-room and then, beyond it, a positively sinfully sybaritic bathroom with a marble jacuzzi bath, gilded mirrors and gold fitments shaped like...mermaids. *Mermaids*? As a child Georgie had been fascinated by fantasy tales of mermaids and unicorns. A peculiar sense of *déjà vu* swept her, a funny little chill running down her taut spinal cord.

'Ees crazy bathroom,' Teresa said almost aggressively, and Georgie spun. 'You like crazy bathroom, *señorita*?'

Georgie moistened her suddenly dry lips with the tip of her tongue and simultaneously caught a glimpse of the wonderful painting on the wall opposite the bed. Unless she was very much mistaken—and closer examination told her she was not—the exquisitely detailed oil portrayed a unicorn in a forest...

Realising that Teresa was still awaiting a reply, Georgie mumbled weakly, 'I like the bathroom, the room...everything, but I feel a little—a little tired.'

'Dinner is served at nine. I send maids to unpack,' Teresa announced with a stiff little nod, and indicated a bell-pull on the wall. 'You wish anything, you call, *señorita*.'

On cottonwool legs, Georgie sank down on the edge of the bed. It was coincidence that the décor should mirror her own taste to such an extent. What else could it be *but* coincidence, for goodness' sake? Kicking off her shoes and dispensing with the coat, Georgie lay down, smothering a yawn. In a minute, she would get up and wash and change and explore. She intended to make the best of this unexpected stay at the *estancia*.

After all, she was on holiday and, had the concept of being grateful to Rafael not been utterly repellent to her, she would have thanked him for making it possible for her to spend at least a few more days abroad.

A lamp was burning by the bed when she woke and the curtains had been drawn. Checking the time, Georgie rose in a hurry. Her pitifully slender wardrobe had been hung in a capacious closet in the dressing-room while she slept and *every* crumpled garment had been ironed as well. A single drawer contained the rest of her clothing and she sighed. Her collection of neat skirts and jackets which she had worn on teaching practice had all been winter-weight and, when it had come to packing for a hot climate, Georgie had had to fall back largely on outfits last worn in Majorca two years earlier on a family holiday. Beachwear, strictly speaking, she conceded, fingering a pair of Lycra shorts with a frown.

She was desperate for a bath but there was only time for a quick shower. Then, donning her one smart outfit, the elegantly cut fine white dress which she had worn for her graduation ceremony, Georgie brushed her rippling mane of curls and dug through her few cosmetics to add some delicate colour to her cheeks and lips. A maid passing through the hall showed her into a formal drawing-room which she found rather oppressive. She was studying a portrait of a forbidding but very handsome man when the door opened behind her.

'You find your accommodation comfortable?'

She turned, her wide hesitant gaze falling on Rafael and, although she had told herself that she would be perfectly composed, her stomach cramped instantly with nerves. The sight of Rafael in a dinner-jacket, a white shirt accentuating the exotic gold of his skin and the darkness of his eyes, took her back in time and she tensed, tearing her attention from him and sliding down on to the nearest seat. 'Very,' she said stiffly.

'What would you like to drink?'

Georgie tensed even more and she was furious with herself for being so over-sensitive. 'Anything,' she muttered.

Taut as a bowstring, she watched him cross the room to a cabinet and listened to the clink of glass. How did he contrive to make her feel that every sentence he spoke to her was a put-down? A someone's-walking-over-my-grave sensation seemed to take over more strongly with every minute she remained in his radius. Angrily, she bent her head. She hated him. Naturally it was a severe strain to be forced to accept his hospitality and feel the need to be at least superficially polite.

Indeed, Georgie only had to think of the damage he had done when she had been at a very impressionable age, and her blood boiled. Rafael's deliberate attempt to reduce her to the level of a promiscuous slut back in her hotel room had simply provided fresh fodder for the bitterness of the past. But it had also brought alive again raw emotions which she had put behind her a long time ago, and she was finding that experience unexpectedly painful.

Right now, she was recalling the staggering response she had given him when he had kissed her, a response she had been too confused even to think about earlier in the day. Now that memory haunted her, shamed her. Four years ago, Rafael had taught her things about herself that, afterwards, she would have given anything to forget. She was a very physical person, or at least she had been with him. In his arms, she had never been in control. She had been entrapped by an uncontrollable passion which made mincemeat of every moral principle Jenny had dinned into her while she was growing up.

Had he so desired, Rafael could have gone to bed with her on the first date and, long after he had gone, Georgie had tortured herself with the fear that that wanton ability to forget everything when he touched her had actually laid the basis of Rafael's cruel misjudgement of her. Angels and whores… Steve's reading of Rafael had often returned to haunt her. And she had told herself that if Rafael was that primitive, she had had a very lucky escape indeed.

But what did she tell herself *now*? How could she have stood there and allowed him to kiss her in that horribly intimate way? She wasn't a besotted teenager any more. Admittedly, she was still sexually inexperienced, she allowed grudgingly, but then, having been scorched as badly by passion as she had been at nineteen, that was not really surprising. So why hadn't she objected to being manhandled this morning?

Because you liked it, a dry little voice put in to her flood of inner turmoil. She froze, her pallor suddenly washed by hot colour. Rafael chose that same moment to slot a tall glass between her nerveless fingers.

'A Tequila Sunrise,' Rafael drawled softly. 'I have an excellent memory and I can only hope that you have no ambition to get seriously sloshed tonight.'

Georgie stared at the glass in stricken horror. The offer of a cup of poison could not have made her feel more threatened. One sip of that mixture and she was convinced she would throw up. His brutality absolutely devastated her. That evening, that ghastly final evening four years ago… Her narrow shoulders clenched as though he had laid a whip across them. The lousy sadist, she thought wildly, burning tears of sheer humiliation lashing her lowered eyelids. If there had been a gun within reach, she would have shot him dead without remorse.

'I see you remember too,' Rafael murmured smoothly.

Georgie threw her head up, a blaze of raw hostility leaping through her veins. She put that glass to her lips and she drank like a sailor on shore-leave after six months of sobriety. In her rage, she tasted nothing. 'Thanks,' she said tautly. 'I needed that!'

'Evidently, you did.' A hard smile curved Rafael's sensual mouth.

If he fondly imagined she was about to hang her head in shame because one time in her life she had got stupidly drunk, he was wrong!

'Do you think there would be time before dinner for another one?' Georgie murmured hopefully, taking up the challenge with a vengeance. If he chose to think that she was a drunk as well as a slut, he was quite free to do so. Anything was better than letting him see that he could still get to her. And displaying a total lack of concern for Rafael's prehistoric ideal of how a 'lady' ought to behave was surely the best way possible to demonstrate her complete indifference to him?

Recalling her own eagerness to please in the past could only make her cringe. All her life she had been extrovert, fiery and opinionated. But Rafael had put a clamp on such emotional excesses, making her feel that to be acceptable she had to tone herself down into a paler version of herself. Afraid that if she couldn't be what he wanted, she would lose him, Georgie had done a very fair imitation of a doormat until inevitably she had begun to resent his arrogant assumption of supremacy.

Another drink arrived. Georgie swallowed hard in a silence that was beginning to slice along her nerve-endings and made herself sip through clenched teeth.

'I have often wished that I had taken you up on your offer that night,' Rafael delivered, fixing brilliant golden eyes to her openly transfixed face. 'But it would have meant breaking every honourable instinct I possessed. I've never made love to a woman under the influence of alcohol before, but with you it would have paid dividends. I would have known then that I wasn't your first lover——'

'And I dare say I would have known that I wasn't yours either!' Georgie slung back at him in growing outrage. In throwing up her reckless behaviour that night, Rafael demonstrated a savage, unashamed desire to humiliate her.

'Naturally not...what would you expect?' Rafael demanded shortly, after a decidedly stunned pause that such an irrelevance as *his* sexual experience should be mentioned. Dark colour accentuated the fierce angles of his hard cheekbones, his handsome mouth a compressed line.

Georgie tossed back another swig of alcohol, well aware she had disconcerted him. 'Oops, to think I had one chance in my entire life to be ravished in a Ferrari and I blew it!' She fluttered her lashes in an attitude of deep regret, beginning to enjoy herself as much as she had thoroughly enjoyed herself in the amateur dramatic society at college. 'That one perfect spontaneous moment missed... But then, you're not a spontaneous kind of guy, are you?'

'Not in a public car park...no,' Rafael breathed in a driven undertone, with more than a suggestion of gritted white teeth to the reply as he studied her with lancing dark eyes. 'I find it hard to believe that you can refer to that night so casually.'

Georgie flicked him a glance, adrenalin fairly roaring through her. A determined smile tilted her mobile mouth as she regarded him from below her thick copper lashes. 'Why not? After all, you weren't the only one deceived four years ago...I was as well.'

'*You* were?' Rafael breathed, with an incredulous expression.

'You put out an impression which you don't deliver,' Georgie sighed. 'I hope you don't mind me being frank——'

Rafael shot her a gilttering glance from the cabinet where he was pouring himself another drink that looked very much like a double. It was good to know she was penetrating that truly enormous ego and puncturing it just a little. 'Feel free...'

Georgie was really getting into her role now. 'Well, you say I was violently in love with you but, frankly, like most teenagers, I was more in love with love. I was also very easily impressed. Your limousine and your accent knocked me sideways and I don't mind admitting it,' she assured him cheerfully. 'But I'd have been just as impressed if you hadn't had a word of English or the ability to voice a single intelligent sentence. I fell in love with my own fanatasies——'

'No doubt you intend to share those with me as well,' Rafael countered with a blazing smile of challenge.

Georgie wrinkled her nose and strove to look coy. 'Only with my lovers... Some men do need a little push in the right direction.'

'I need no push.'

That was getting just a bit too close to the bone for Georgie and she blinked rapidly, her cheeks colouring. 'How fascinating,' she said, in a deliberately unfascinated voice.

'What is this impression which I put out and didn't deliver?' Rafael enquired silkily.

'I really don't think I should say. My big mouth,' Georgie groaned, as he settled yet another glass into her hand. 'It's such a long time ago——'

'But I insist.'

'Well...you see, I expected you to be...' Georgie licked at her taut lower lip and her eyes collided involuntarily with incandescent golden ones that were nailed to her with relentless force and, not surprisingly, that alarming collision silenced her.

'You expected me to be what?' Rafael demanded with flaring impatience.

'I expected you to live up to your bad reputation...but you didn't,' Georgie imparted with unhidden venom. 'I expected you to be incredibly passionate and sexy...and, frankly, you were a disappointment——'

'I was so much of a disappointment, you came to me and you begged me to take you back,' Rafael slotted in, hooded eyes showing a mere glimmer of gleaming gold below the inky black luxuriance of his lashes. 'You wept and you pleaded and you lied...'

Georgie turned white, stared down into her untouched glass, slaughtered utterly by the reminder of her lowest hour. 'And it was like taking the cure,' she whispered between clenched teeth. 'So much for love. It died there and then and I'm happy to tell you that I've never fancied myself in love since.'

'Love has nothing to do with what is between us.'

Her knuckles showed white as she tightened her grip on her glass. 'There is nothing between us.'

'Look at me and tell me that—show the courage of your conviction,' Rafael derided.

Georgie felt as though she was being torn apart. Just minutes earlier she had been playing games with him but that false bravado had now deserted her. She felt cornered, intimidated, suddenly knew that she had been very naïve indeed to allow him to bring her to the *estancia*, even more naïve to imagine that he would play the polite host to her role of guest.

'I said...look at me.'

The command, given by a male accustomed to absolute authority, sent her tension climbing to meteoric heights. A lean hand removed the glass from her convulsed grip. Powerful fingers closed round her forearm, literally forcing her upright, and instantly she attempted to pull away.

'Stop it,' Rafael commanded rawly, scanning her drawn face with scorchingly angry dark eyes. 'Do you think I enjoy wanting you? Do you think I am proud of the desire you arouse in me? But this time I will not walk away. Why should I? Why shouldn't I take what I want? You owe me...'

Georgie was trembling, shaken by the force of anger she had unleashed. 'I owe you nothing, not even the time of day!'

'But you'll still give me everything,' he assured her.

'Never!' Georgie vowed. 'And stop threatening me!'

'Do you feel threatened when I make love to you?' With a husky sound of very male amusement, Rafael drew her closer and ran an insolently expert hand down over the full curve of her breasts and she shuddered helplessly.

'Don't touch me!' On the edge of panic, Georgie sought to break free of his hold as a blunt forefinger circled the erect bud of a nipple, visibly thrusting through the thin fabric of her dress. A quivering, hateful excitement leapt into being inside her but she fought it to the last ditch.

'Do all your lovers turn you on this hard and this fast?' Rafael lowered his dark head and allowed the tip of his tongue to slide erotically between her lips, just once, in a darting foray that sent heat coursing through her in a debilitating wave.

'Every one of them!' she slammed back in a breathless rush.

'But I'll be the one you remember long after I'm gone,' Rafael completed with predatory assurance, quite untouched by her attempt to repel him, a strong hand splaying across her hips to jerk her into even closer contact, and she stopped breathing altogether as he moved fluidly against her, bringing her into unashamed contact with the hard thrust of his arousal.

Her treacherous body was on fire and she closed her eyes, struggling to think, struggling not to react. 'No,' she whispered shakily.

He lifted her with ease and one of her shoes fell off. She opened startled eyes a split-second before he brought his mouth crashing down on hers. She stopped thinking, she started simply feeling. The effect was that immediate. Her hands bit into his broad shoulders as she strained against the hard heat of his muscular length. Her fingers drifted into his hair and she was lost, controlled by an intolerable need that sent the blood pounding at an insane rate through her veins. Slowly, very slowly, he slid her down the length of his body on to her feet again and lifted his head.

'You go to pieces when I touch you. I like that... I love that,' Rafael muttered with a ragged groan of satisfaction. 'It gives me an incredible sexual high no other woman has ever matched. I saw you lying asleep in that cell and every decent thought, every piece of self-restraint fled instantaneously. I'd have killed to get you out of there and into my bed.'

Finding herself lop-sided, minus one shoe, Georgie crouched down in a dazed and trembling search to locate the missing item. That she couldn't think straight didn't help. But then, Rafael was proving a whole lot harder to handle than she could ever have imagined. She didn't know Rafael as a lover. In that field, she didn't know Rafael at all. And in this mood, Rafael was a revelation, a distinctly intimidating revelation. Nothing she had read, nothing she had ever heard, could save her from feeling gruesomely out of her own limited depth.

'What are you doing?' Rafael enquired huskily.

He pressed her back on a nearby sofa, produced her shoe and proceeded to slide it back on, but he didn't get back up again. He smoothed his lean hands slowly up over her slender calves to her knees, watching her intently from beneath indolently lowered black lashes that a woman would have killed to possess.

'Dinner,' Georgie said jerkily, every muscle tightening in stricken response.

'Dinner is served when I ring,' Rafael leant forward and brushed his mouth very softly across hers, his breath fanning her cheek as long fingers pushed her knees gently apart. *'Dios mío...'* he murmured softly, letting his tongue probe smoothly between her lips and making her shake like leaf in a high wind, a tiny whisper of shaken protest escaping her throat. 'Food to die for, clothes to die for... your expression. This has to be sex to die for.'

'No,' she mumbled, but she opened her mouth for his exploration, shivering as the intrusion became less playful.

'Why are you so tense?' Caressing fingers slid below the hem of her dress, stroking along the tender skin of her inner thigh, forcing a stifled gasp to erupt from her.

'T-Tense?'

'Surely it has not been that long since a man made love to you?'

Her hands were in his hair, and she didn't honestly know how they had got there. One half of her was petrified, the other half of her was mesmerised by what he was doing to her. 'Forever.' Her voice was a thin thread of barely recognisable sound.

She clashed with devouring golden eyes, drowned as though time had stopped, leaving her in limbo. Never in the twenty-three years of her existence had she experienced anything even approaching what she was feeling now. He was barely touching her and her entire body was in meltdown. The intensity of her own arousal devastated her every attempt to regain her hold on a situation which had moved with incredible rapidity out of her control.

'*Por Dios*...I want you so badly it hurts,' he muttered fiercely, raking a single fingertip across the tautly stretched scrap of lace covering the very heart of her, jolting every bone in her body with an intolerable rush of erotic sensation.

Somebody banged on the door. In fact, somebody banged on the door so loudly that Georgie very nearly hit the ceiling in shock. Far less susceptible to the disturbance, Rafael dragged shimmering golden eyes from her and sprang fluidly upright. Georgie swallowed hard and rearranged her hemline with trembling hands.

'We will eat,' Rafael murmured flatly.

Hectically flushed, and barely able to stand on legs that were wobbling with shock, Georgie espied Teresa in the doorway and, if possible, felt her blush spread down to encompass every other part of her exposed body. A dark, deep hole to hide in would have been extraordinarily welcome. Saved in the very nick of time by the housekeeper, she thought, on the quivering edge of hysteria.

She made it into the palatial dining-room and down onto a chair. Inside her head pounded a relentless refrain. How could you be so stupid...how could you be so weak? What was she, some sort of brainless puppet? Was she so over-sexed that she couldn't say no like any other decent woman? What did it say about her that after all the insults, all the cruelty, she had still allowed Rafael to touch her?

Rafael said something sharp in Spanish, ice dripping off every syllable. Teresa retreated at speed.

'You don't seem to get on very well with your housekeeper.'

'She does not approve of your presence here. But what I do in my own home is entirely my affair.' Rafael shook out a white linen napkin with an air of magnificent unconcern. 'Teresa does not know whether to save you or condemn you. The taxing question of whether you are a virtuous woman being wickedly seduced, or a shameless hussy, will no doubt keep her awake all night. But by tomorrow the truth will out. She will decide that you are beyond saving and that I am no better and no worse than any other man in giving way to temptation. Then peace will be restored to my household!'

Frozen, with a spoon hovering indecisively over the very tempting fruit concoction set before her, Georgie cleared her throat. 'What truth will out?'

'That we are lovers.'

'I am not going to sleep with you!' Darkened violet eyes flared furiously down the table at him.

'I hope not. Sleep does not feature anywhere in my expectations of the night ahead,' Rafael delivered lazily, lifting his wine-glass and resting back in his chair to survey her with slumbrous dark eyes. He toasted her with a graceful movement of one brown hand. '*Salud* . . . to every fantasy being fulfilled. Sadly, the Ferrari is in London, but I don't lack imagination in the bedroom and I doubt very much that you will be disappointed.'

Georgie tossed aside her spoon, any idea of eating now abandoned. 'If you think for one moment that I intend to allow you to use me——' she returned in seething indigation.

'But I intend to reciprocate in being used,' Rafael interrupted mockingly, but there was a current of something distinctly more menacing in the assurance. 'Our hunger is mutual, but I have never had a purely sexual affair before. If I'm a little clumsy sometimes, remember that. I don't quite know how to treat you. Perhaps that is because the minute I take my hands off you, I see your every flaw... then I wonder what the hell I'm doing with you.'

Georgie flew upright, her facial muscles rigid, her beautiful eyes aflame with fury. 'I want to return to my hotel tomorrow!'

'No way,' Rafael said softly. 'You go when I say it is time, not before.'

Georgie lifted her glass and stalked down the length of the polished table. With a flick of her wrist, she tossed the contents in his face. 'But *I* say it is time now, and I expect you to listen.'

A hand snaked out and trapped her fingers, preventing her retreat. Calmly he dried himself with a napkin while retaining that punishing grip on her. Only then did he turn blazing dark eyes on her furiously flushed profile. 'It really hasn't dawned on you yet, has it?' he demanded, jerking her round so that she had to face him. 'You bounce through life like an exuberant, destructive child—undisciplined, wholly self-centred and greedy, careless of the damage you cause, never counting the cost. But today is the day you start paying for being a shallow, opportunistic little bitch.'

Georgie stared back at him in stunned disbelief. 'You're—you're out of your mind...' she whispered.

'No,' Rafael murmured softly, silkily, 'I'm the kind of unforgiving bastard you wouldn't find in your worst nightmares. And you really don't know why, do you?'

'I think you're acting like someone unhinged,' she muttered helplessly.

'I was very unhinged four years ago,' Rafael agreed, his fingers tightening so savagely on hers that her smaller hand was crushed. He threw his handsome dark head back and studied her with unflinching intensity, his eloquent mouth hardening. 'Take a good long look at those rooms upstairs. Take a note of the severe lack of good taste in that Hollywood film-star bathroom. Ask yourself who you know with a vulgar penchant for mermaid taps and marble. And then ask yourself why I would have wasted an obscene amount of money actually paying someone to make them.'

Transfixed by the savage onslaught of his biting dark eyes, Georgie's stomach cramped up. She couldn't feel her hand any more but she was beyond that awareness. She couldn't breathe, couldn't move, because she was paralysed by what he was telling her, unable to credit that her insanely confused thoughts could be heading in the right direction. 'I—I . . .' And for the life of her, she couldn't think of what to say.

'That suite was decorated for my bride—for my beautiful, *pure* bride.' Rafael drew her bruised fingers to his mouth and kissed them in a scathing demonstration of derision before dropping her hand again.

'You wanted to marry me?' Georgie demanded starkly, her voice cracking loudly in the charged silence.

'You really didn't know... I always wondered.' Rafael vented a grimly amused laugh as he read the sheer astonishment in her dazed eyes. 'But then, how *could* you know how to deal with a man who treated you with respect? Naturally, I did not want to make love to you before our wedding-night, but that restraint on my part was not appreciated. You got bored, didn't you?'

Every scrap of pink had drained from Georgie's vibrantly beautiful face. 'No...no!' she said again shakily.

'So you went to bed with someone else—someone wise enough to know that the very last thing you wanted was respect—another teenager.' All the raw savagery of Rafael's *conquistador* ancestry was stamped into the harsh lines of his golden features, his embittered fury starkly apparent in his blazing stare. 'I, Rafael Rodriguez Berganza, made to look a fool by a teenage boy!'

Trembling, Georgie whispered jerkily, 'Danny was a friend, nothing more——'

Rafael reached out and curved a cruelly strong hand round her elbow, forcing her closer. 'You think that makes a difference? That it meant nothing to you, that it was a drunken one-night stand which I was never intended to know about? I always knew that! But was it worth it? I ask you now, *querida mía* was it worth what you lost? Looking at you now, I would say not,' he derided, thrusting her back from him with contempt. 'Because you still want me. You still want me so much it terrifies you... and if you had had any intelligence at all, you would have known yourself safer in that prison cell than you are here with me!'

Georgie backed away. 'I don't like being threatened!' she spat back at him in a tempest of emotion too tangled for her even to comprehend. All she could recognise was the terrible rage which dominated her every other reaction. 'And I didn't want to marry you anyway! My idea of marriage is not being told what to do from dawn to dusk and getting the big freeze when you fail... and my ideal partner is not some international playboy, who sleeps with every woman he wants and then thinks he's got some God-given right to marry a virgin!'

Rafael plunged upright. 'I did not think it my right——'

'No, evidently you selected me at school and hoped to God you'd got me in time!' Georgie slung back in disgust. 'You know something? You are everything Steve ever said you were. Primitive, backward and bigoted.'

Rafael froze and shot her a seething look of such frightening anger that her voice simply died away. 'You say that name once more in my presence and I will surely kill you...'

Georgie spun on her heel and took off through the dining-room like a rocket. She flew up the stairs, raced across the landing and slammed breathlessly into her bedroom. Then she flung herself on the bed in the darkness and burst into helpless floods of tears.

CHAPTER FOUR

A GOOD cry was supposed to be therapeutic. Georgie peered at herself through swollen eyes half an hour later, acknowledged the tumultuous state of her jangling nerves and distraught emotions, and decided dully that the good cry had utterly failed.

Teresa was hovering with a large laden tray when Georgie walked back into the bedroom. She aimed an uncertain smile at Georgie, but Georgie was so embarrassed by her red, puffy face that she lowered her head.

'You have dinner, *señorita*?'

'Thanks.' Distress hadn't killed Georgie's appetite. But then, food had been pretty thin on the ground over the past forty-eight hours.

Forty-eight hours, she reflected sickly. That swine had all but wiped her out in little more than twelve hours! Yet, four years ago, Rafael had actually planned to marry her! Finding out that now shook her rigid. Pick a teenage bride and mould her like unformed clay into the correct image... She hadn't been rich or well-born but, heaven knew, she had been malleable! And Rafael must have wanted her; Rafael must very badly have wanted her, she decided dazedly, to overlook all her other deficiencies.

For a few minutes, Georgie hugged that new knowledge to her. It shed a different light on that long-ago summer, briefly mollified her damaged pride. Then, with protective parents hovering, not to mention her youth and close friendship with his sister, he hadn't had that many options, she conceded ruefully. How could he have

59

embarked on an affair with her? There would always have been the risk that she might tell María Cristina when it was over. And how did you have an affair with a girl who had to be home by midnight unless her stepbrother was in tow? A choky little laugh escaped Georgie. Was that why he had gone up in flames at the mere mention of Steve?

It would be foolish to deny that her parents had been worried by Rafael's interest in her, their concern exacerbated by Steve, who had slated the idea that Rafael could be trusted with their precious daughter. Throughout those weeks with Rafael, Georgie had been irritated by Steve's attitude, but she had grudgingly conceded his genuine concern that she was going to be badly hurt.

And when Steve's expectations had been fulfilled, Georgie had been grateful for his smooth and careless dismissal of their parents' astonishment that her relationship with Rafael had been so abruptly concluded. In fact, that understated kindness in shielding her from awkward questions had helped Georgie more than anything else to forget her stepbrother's disturbing behaviour on that final night.

She shivered, for she liked to recall that least of all. But, whether she liked it or not, the events of that catastrophic evening were flooding back to her. Did she blame everything on the amount of alcohol she had recklessly consumed? No, she could not allow that excuse. And, even without Steve's encouragement, she would have rebelled against Rafael's arrogance sooner or later.

She remembered Steve's girlfriend, a very pretty girl, only a couple of years her senior. It had been the first time she had met Janet. But that evening she had noticed how very careless Steve was of Janet's feelings. He hadn't paid her much attention. It had been a new view of Steve which she hadn't liked. It had made her wonder if all men were like that. Once a man knew you loved him, did you then become boring?

Georgie had been so much on edge that night, conscious that Rafael had been disturbingly distant on the last two occasions she had been with him. She had felt threatened and insecure and she had simultaneously despised herself for being so weak. She had told herself that if Rafael was getting bored with her, she could handle it. But she hadn't handled it. She had got childishly, stupidly drunk.

'I'm taking you home,' Rafael had told her grimly.

'If you take her home in that state, my stepfather will kill her!' Steve had protested.

'As opposed to me killing her?' Rafael had drawled with flat indifference. 'I'll take her home to her father and let him do it. Will that make you happy?'

Steve had become abusive. Rafael had ignored him and dragged Georgie out to his car. She hadn't wanted to go home. At that point, the evening had gone totally haywire. She had started to scream at Rafael in the Ferrari, and it was amazing how much she had said that later, she had to acknowledge, had truly come from the heart. Alcohol had filled her with the Dutch courage to list her every resentment.

'I thought you were more mature. Now I face reality—the inescapable gap between hope and self-delusion,' Rafael had commented very drily. 'Then, how do I blame you? One does not rob the schoolroom and expect to be rewarded with an adult. But, right now, I feel that I robbed the nursery department!'

Georgie had subsided like a pricked balloon but she had been wildly confused by the unfamilair strength of the emotions tearing her apart. One minute she loved him, the next she felt she hated him. And when he talked down to her like that, hatred rose uppermost.

But he had rewarded her sullen silence with a kiss, yet another in a long line of fleeting salutes, as if she was in very truth, the child he accused her of being. Still, there had not been an ounce of the passion she craved. And she had wanted so badly to prove that she was a woman, a *real* woman capable of satisfying his every adult desire.

And maybe she had also been trying to convince herself that she in turn had some power over him. So what had she done? Even four years after the event, Georgie cringed from recalling the fact that she had shamelessly thrown herself at Rafael in the car, employing every atom of wanton encouragement she had ever read about in racy female magazine articles of the 'How to hang on to your man' variety.

And it had worked . . . briefly. Rafael had uttered a ragged groan. With satisfying speed, all that infuriating restraint of his had vanished. She had ended up flat on the passenger seat, his mouth hotly sealed to hers, his body hard and demanding, crushing her yielding curves, all the red-hot passion she had for him finally matched. It hadn't even occurred to her that they were in a public car park. Georgie had been beyond such trivialities. But then Rafael had sworn viciously in Spanish and thrust himself back from her, an unholy glitter in his dark probing gaze.

'Who taught you how to arouse a man?' he had demanded, without hesitation ablaze with suspicion and distrust.

He hadn't been impressed by her stammered assurance that nobody had taught her anything. Georgie had been eaten alive by mortification. In the end she had been in such a state of sobbing incoherence that when she had seen Steve crossing the car park she had leapt out of the Ferrari and raced after him.

Steve had had a row with Janet, who had already gone home in a taxi. He had taken Georgie back to his house, sooner than subject her to the horror of facing her father in the condition she was in. And then her nightmare evening had taken its second very bad turn for the worse... in many ways, at the time, the very worst turn of all.

Georgie paced the richly carpeted floor, recalling with a shudder how she had felt when Steve had, without any prior warning that she had noticed, switched from understanding big brother to would-be lover. He had had a comforting arm round her shoulders as they walked into the lounge and then he had suddenly grabbed her and begun kissing her! Georgie had been shattered and repelled. Steve might not be her real brother, but she had always regarded him in the asexual guise of one. His forceful embrace might only have lasted a short time but it had shocked and frightened Georgie as much as attempted rape.

'Hell, I'm *not* your brother... don't look at me like that!' Steve had shouted at her before she escaped upstairs to lock herself in the bathroom and be horribly sick.

He had tried to talk to her through the door. He had had too much to drink. He was upset about Janet. Couldn't she understand? But that night Georgie hadn't been capable of understanding. She had shrunk from the challenge of opening that door and facing him again. And when Steve had told her that he was going out to check that he had locked his car, Georgie had fled through the back door.

She had gone to Danny's apartment, hadn't been able to think of any other place to run, would certainly not have turned to Rafael after the treatment he had meted out earlier. Danny had given her his bed and slept on the lounge sofa. Georgie had been so upset, he really hadn't known what to do with her. In the end he had just made her a cup of coffee and left her in peace.

The next morning, raised voices had wakened her. She had sat up, naked in the tumbled bed, to find Rafael standing in the bedroom doorway in a sort of seething silent rage of incredulity. Without a word he had swung on his heel and stridden back out of the flat. Danny had appeared then, shivering wet and dripping from the shower, still wrapped in a bath-towel. 'He just forced his way in...' he had mumbled. 'And he's a lot bigger than I am. Hope you didn't mind me making myself scarce.'

Steve had been their second visitor, close on Rafael's heels. Georgie hadn't been able to meet her stepbrother's eyes.

'How did Rafael know where I was?' she had demanded.

'I guessed you had to be here and I told him.' Steve had sighed. 'I thought you'd want to see him and smooth over that stupid row you had with him.'

And, of course, had Rafael not completely misinterpreted what he had seen, she would indeed have been glad to see him.

Steve had bent over backwards to make peace with her, fervently apologising for upsetting her the night before. He had papered over the cracks of her discomfiture, made it easier for her to try and pretend that nothing had changed between them. But it had, she acknowledged sadly. A new distance had gradually eroded their once close ties.

Later that day, when she had approached Rafael, it had not initially occurred to Georgie that Rafael might not listen to her. She had been incredibly naïve in her assumption that Rafael would believe her when she explained that things might have *looked* suspicious at Danny's but that in actuality everything had been entirely innocent. But then, she had naturally assumed that Rafael knew her well enough to have *some* degree of trust in her...

She had put his ridiculous suspicions in the Ferrari down to her own childish behaviour and mutually frayed tempers. Indeed, travelling up in the lift to Rafael's penthouse apartment, Georgie had been so far removed from reality that she had been happily thinking that Rafael must have been jealous and that jealousy had to mean he *cared*. And, right now, remembering that piece of inane stupidity made Georgie want to tear her hair out and scream. That day she had been a lamb to the slaughter.

But never again, she reminded herself doggedly and, since sleep was the last thing on her over-active mind, she stripped, filled the marble bath with hot water and bubbles and climbed in to wash her hair and then lie back and thoughtfully survey the mermaid taps. For her benefit... Incredible. When, when had he done all this? And how had everything contrived to go so badly wrong? Her throat ached. Running a flannel under the cold tap, she draped it irritably across her still reddened eyes.

Rafael had fallen off his pedestal with a resounding crash. First love—nothing more painful, nothing more intense. It was those memories which saddened her, not any sense of loss or regret. The marriage would have been a disaster. Like Desdemona but without the saintliness, she conceded ruefully, she might have ended up murdered by her enraged and jealous husband. Rafael hadn't trusted her one inch.

She could not have been the wife his intelligence would have chosen. Perhaps it had been the awareness that they were temperamentally unsuited which had made him seize on the escape-clause supplied by her supposed fling with Danny. Rafael had not had grounds to judge her that harshly. He had known how much she loved him. How could he have seriously believed that after one stupid row she would jump into bed with a boy almost a year younger than she was? What kind of sense did that make?

'I knew you wouldn't be able to resist the bath...'

Tearing the flannel from her eyes in shock, Georgie reeled up into a sitting position, water sloshing noisily everywhere. 'What the hell are you doing in here?' she gasped in outrage.

Rafael angled a splintering smile over her startled features and laughed with genuine amusement. 'You're such a curious mixture, Georgie. Puritan and sybarite.' His dinner-jacket hooked in one hand, his white silk dress-shirt undone at his brown throat, he sat down on the edge of the bath. 'You radiate conflicting signals which confuse. Looking at you now, I see why I was taken in four years ago. That look of shock and indignation is very impressive, but the way you're hugging your knees is decided overkill,' he murmured silkily, surveying her with glittering golden eyes. 'You have a very beautiful body... why hide it?'

'Get out of here!' Georgie sizzled back at him furiously.

He tugged a fleecy towel off the rail just out of her reach and extended it with a faintly derisive smile. 'Then you've already learnt that a little mystique is more stimulating than a floor-show?'

Georgie snatched at the towel and wrapped it clumsily round herself as she stood up, her cheeks burning hotly. 'I want you to leave,' she told him stiffly, striving for a note of command and dignity.

Rafael flung his ebony head back and laughed spontaneously.

Georgie stood there, violet eyes flashing with rage. 'Look, I have got the message that you consider yourself absolutely irresistible, but I've made it clear that I am not interested!'

'Where was I?' Rafael prompted.

'Where were you when?' Georgie snapped.

Rafael slid fluidly upright. 'Where was I when you were making it very clear that you were not interested?' he enquired lethally.

Georgie's teeth clenched. 'Look, I just want to go back to La Paz and sort out my passport!'

'You are really running scared.' Sensual dark eyes scanned her shrewdly. 'Why is that? Pride?'

'I don't know what you're talking about.' Georgie stepped out of the bath.

He reached for her without warning, curving two powerful arms round her and sweeping her off her feet. 'I won't let you run.'

'Put me down, for heaven's sake!' Georgie shrieked.

'No.'

He stared down at her, golden eyes meshing with violet. Her own heartbeat thundered slowly, heavily through her body, stretching every tiny nerve taut. 'Rafael...'

'You burn for me... you can't hide that,' he told her. 'I see it in your eyes, in the way you move, in the very voice you use when you speak to me.'

'So you attract me... so what?' Georgie dared in desperation. 'We don't all follow our most basic instincts!'

'But you do... all the time. However, here you will follow your most basic instincts for my benefit alone,' Rafael asserted, settling her down on the bed and dropping down beside her in one powerful movement. 'No strings on either side, no lies, no misunderstandings. We share a bed, nothing more.'

The hectic pink in her cheeks had receded, leaving her pale. He was peeling off his silk shirt to reveal the bronzed breadth of his shoulders and the curling black triangle of hair hazing his pectoral muscles. As though impelled by a force outside her control, Georgie's unwittingly fascinated gaze lingered and she swallowed hard. On one level she couldn't believe that she was actually in a bedroom on a bed with Rafael. It felt so *unreal*.

'If you touch me, I'll scream blue murder!'

'What a novel promise,' Rafael breathed huskily, winding long brown fingers into her tangled damp hair as she attempted to sit up and preventing the movement.

'Now just back off before this gets embarrassing for both of us!' Georgie hissed up at him. 'If I scream, your servants will come running!'

'We are alone in the house.'

As he lowered his weight down on to hers, Georgie froze, and stared up at him with darkened violet eyes. 'We can't be...'

'We are.' He bent over her and nipped playfully at her lower lip with the kind of sensual expertise she was defenceless against, the tip of his tongue following gently in the wake of the tiny pain to further inflame. 'I have waited so long to see you on this bed in this room,' he confessed. 'And when it's over, when you're gone, everything will be ripped out and these rooms will be renovated. It will be as though you never existed——'

The assurance dug sudden fear into her bones, banishing her momentary loss of concentration. Georgie put up her hands and hit out at him with raw hostility. With a stifled imprecation, he anchored both her hands to the sheet and gazed down at her with incandescent golden eyes, his strong jawline clenching as he absorbed the apprehension in her upturned gaze.

'*Por Dios*...why should you fear me?' he demanded abruptly, releasing her wrists.

Trembling, Georgie thrust him away from her and sat up, clutching with desperate hands at the bath-towel's dipping edge across her full breasts. It was a kind of fear he could never have understood, for he would not have believed its source. She was afraid of herself *and* him. 'I just want you to l-leave me alone!' she muttered shakily.

He murmured something soft in his own language and pulled her close. Stiffening, she shivered violently as the towel lurched dangerously downward. 'No!' she gasped, panicking.

'*Sí...*' Rafael countered, choosing to gather her even closer and cover her lips hungrily with his. The towel slipped; she didn't notice, but a tiny gasp was torn from her as her taut nipples were abraided by his hair-roughened chest.

She was electrified by the way he was making love to her mouth. He searched out every sensitive spot and explored it, making the breath rasp in her throat. It felt so good, indeed, it felt so incredibly exciting that she clutched him with her hands, seduced by her own helpless response. As he settled her smoothly back against the crisp white sheet, she was overwhelmed by the sheer welter of sensation that attacked her when he sealed every virile inch of his lean, powerful body to hers.

He stared down at her with a raw, sexual hunger that burned through clear to her bones. Heat flooded her in a blinding surge. A hard thigh sank between hers and she quivered violently, the fevered pulse-point of desire thrumming ever higher inside her.

'You see...' Rafael muttered thickly. 'And I haven't even begun yet.'

As he buried his mouth in a tiny hollow below her fragile collarbone, he let his thumbs rub expertly across her thrusting pink nipples. She jerked, an involuntary moan torn from her, and he lowered his head to employ his mouth and that wickedly knowing tongue on those unbearaby sensitive buds. He drove her crazy. Sensation like white-hot lightning licked at every nerve-ending and she twisted and gasped in helpless excitement. She was in thrall to a dark enchantment of the senses and the most extraordinary pleasure.

Her fingers dug into the thick silky depths of his hair and tightened as he sucked a swollen nipple into his mouth. 'Rafael...oh, God, Rafael...' she moaned, out of control and burning up.

Through passion-glazed eyes she focused on him, the darkness of his head against her pale skin, the gold of his hands shaping her treacherously responsive flesh. Her palms moved restively over the satin-smooth muscles in his shoulders and then her fingertips drove into his hair again as her heavy eyelids slid down. There was an ache between her thighs, an absolutely unbearable ache. Her teeth clenched. She wanted, needed...

He slid up and twisted a hand painfully into her hair as he devoured her mouth again, bruising her lips but answering her every unspoken need. She kissed him back with wild passion, trembling all over, lost in the depths of her own excruciating excitement. He moaned something raggedly in Spanish, cupping her cheekbones, meeting that passion with a savagery that dominated, drove, demanded...

'*Tentadora...bruja,*' Rafael groaned, and then he tensed ever so slightly.

At first Georgie didn't hear the faint buzzing somewhere in the background. Rafael's fingertips were roaming through the damp tangle of curls at the apex of her thighs and she was on a knife-edge of tormented pleasure, quivering skittishly, unable to stay still as he suddenly crushed her mouth beneath his again. And then, with quite paralysing abruptness, he released her and sprang off the bed.

'Rafael?' she mumbled.

'The phone,' he grated.

'What phone?' And then she heard it, buzzing away somewhere like an angry bee.

'My private line—it must be an emergency. *Dios*,' Rafael swore, shooting her a torn-in-two glance of dark smouldering hunger and incredulous frustration.

Georgie only managed to focus on him as he strode back out of the bathroom, retrieving a mobile phone from his dinner-jacket. And then she got the full effect of Rafael, stark naked. Her lower lip dropped as she stared, for she had no recollection of him removing the rest of his clothes. Sheer shock grabbed her by the throat. Gulping, Georgie took in his uninhibited stance several feet away, not a centimetre of his magnificent golden physique concealed from her. Her gaze wandered on a compulsive journey of its own and absorbed with frank alarm her first sight of a rampantly aroused male. She reddened to the roots of her hair.

'One minute... I promise you, *querida*,' Rafael murmured with erotic emphasis as he surveyed her with blatant male anticipation.

Georgie hauled the sheet over her shamelessly exposed flesh. She started to shake. Aftershock. I am wanton, she thought in a sudden agony of self-reproach. Desire still ached inside her and she was too honest to deny the fact. Rafael had told her that they didn't even need to like each other and she had refused to believe that. But Rafael, veteran of many more such encounters than she, had known better.

From below her lashes, she watched him turn away from her, sounding oddly taut and then breaking into an apparently animated flood of Spanish. You are everything he called you, a nasty little inner voice insisted. She buried her burning face in the pillow. No, she wasn't. Who had ever heard of a promiscuous virgin? But with Rafael her blood ran hot enough to burn her alive. Although right now that same blood was freezing in her veins, because she realised how very close she had come to surrendering her body to a male who despised her.

Yet she wanted him just the way he said she did. Helplessly, instinctively, as though on some frightening subconscious level he had stamped her as his four years ago and her body alone knew it and accepted that reality. Sex, she decided wretchedly, was a primal hunger that respected no boundaries. Rafael Rodriguez Berganza should be the very last male alive capable of awakening her most basic urges. And yet he did, he *did*. On every primitive, physical level, Rafael drew her slavishly to her own destruction. Evidently sexual desire required nothing more intellectual.

'Georgie...'

For a split-second she couldn't face him, and she had to force herself to roll back, push her hair out of her eyes and look at him. She was intensely relieved to see that he was already half dressed. Brilliant dark eyes rested on her with paint-stripping intensity. He reached for his shirt, a wolfish smile hardening his sensual mouth.

'*Perdone*...but we must postpone our pleasure,' he imparted with slumbrous mockery. 'That was Antonio on the phone. María Cristina has given birth to a son and the task of spreading the good news among our many relatives falls on me.'

Astonishment filled Georgie's eyes. 'María Cristina has had her baby? But surely she wasn't due for another couple——'

'He came a little early, but both mother and baby are well. There were no complications,' Rafael assured her, and slowly expelled his breath, a softer light than she had ever seen briefly gentling his strong dark features. 'But I understand they barely made it to the hospital in time! A little boy...' His chiselled jawline clenched and he cast her a sardonic glance. 'He is to be called George.'

His pronounced relief that María Cristina had come through childbirth safely, and the open emotion with which he contemplated his nephew's arrival in the world, twisted something painfully inside Georgie, reminding her just how close were the ties between brother and sister. Then she caught his final statement and her eyes widened. 'She remembered ... She called him after me?' she gasped, tickled pink by the announcement. 'Gosh, I can't wait to see him——'

'But you won't unless my sister chooses to travel to London,' Rafael cut in harshly, his change of mood brutally swift. 'By the time she flies home next week, you will be long gone.'

Losing her short-lived animation, Georgie stilled. Reality had never been less welcome. She collided with his cold dark scrutiny, and her stomach clenched painfully under the onslaught of that unashamed snub. She felt sick with shame, remembering their intimacy brief minutes earlier.

'Is that clear?' Rafael persisted, with what she felt to be quite unnecessary cruelty.

Two years earlier, she had missed out on her best friend's wedding. María Cristina had asked her to be one of her bridesmaids and it had almost broken Georgie's heart to refuse, for her parents had been willing to dig into their savings to make the trip possible for her. She had been afraid of running into Rafael again, although at the time she had not admitted that fear to herself. Her end-of-term exams had been just around the corner and she had used them as an excuse. But this time—*this time*, she told herself with sudden ferocity— she would not play the coward.

'I'll do what I want,' she said tightly, and studied him, a tempestuous gleam in her bitter stare. 'You can't make me leave Bolivia.'

'But you cannot stay here.'

'I'll have money sent out from home,' she threw back. 'I don't care if I have to sleep on the street but I am not leaving without seeing María Cristina and George.'

'I will not allow it,' Rafael drawled in a tone of forbidding finality.

Hunched below her sheet, rawly conscious of her lack of clothing, Georgie sent him a look of naked loathing. 'I want transport out of here tomorrow... do you hear me?'

Rafael dealt her a glittering glance of hard amusement. 'No transport available. You don't leave until I want you to leave, and that won't be until I am finished with you.'

'I'm finished now... I've had enough,' Georgie launched at him with a sob of rage in her shaking voice. 'If you don't get me back to La Paz fast, I'll make you very sorry!'

Rafael lifted his dinner-jacket and viewed her with an insulting lack of concern. 'And how do you plan to do that?'

'Wouldn't you just love to know?'

'I would, indeed. Are you always this childish when you are thwarted?'

'I am not childish!' Georgie spat back, raising her burnished head so that her hair tumbled like tongues of flame in the lamplight. 'If you keep me here against my will, that is an offence... you're breaking the law!'

'But here I *am* the law,' Rafael told her gently.

'I'll be six feet under the day I accept that!' Georgie slung back truthfully.

'No... you'll very probably be under me,' he murmured silkily.

'How dare you?' Georgie's hot temper simply boiled over. 'There's a whole lot of ways I can get even, so don't push me! I can tell tales to María Cristina! I can go home and scream rape and kidnapping!'

'And what proof will you have? These are empty threats. If you had any real affection for my sister, you would not wish to upset her but, even if you did,' Rafael countered very drily, 'she would not believe me capable of such behaviour. As for rape, there has never been any question of force. Kidnapping? You came here willingly as my guest.'

The door thudded shut in his wake and she shuddered with frustration, inflamed by her inability to pierce his tough hide. It was slowly sinking in on her that Rafael hadn't been joking when he had said that she stayed until he chose to let her go. But she still found that incredibly hard to accept. Rafael was an outstandingly well-educated man with a brilliant intellect, outwardly the very epitome of cultured sophistication.

He spoke half a dozen languages fluently, oversaw a vast and flourishing business empire spread across the globe, and still found time to lend considerable support to several international charities, not to mention his environmental interests and the numerous philanthropic projects which made the Berganza name revered on the world stage . . . and this was the man now telling her that she was a prisoner in his home until such time as he satisfied his desire for revenge?

Little wonder that she was feeling confused. But revenge was Rafael's aim. He had brought her here to the *estancia* and put her in the bedroom she would have occupied as his wife. Her stomach lurched sickly as she recalled his assurance that when she was gone these rooms would be stripped, every reminder of her eradicated forever. But, before he reached that dramatic and gothic conclusion, Rafael intended to possess her body in the very same bed in which she would have lain as his bride. Her skin literally chilled as she saw the savage parody he desired to enact to slake his macho pride of

the slur she had cast on it four years ago by her apparent
betrayal.

As his bride, she would have been treated with respect
and tenderness. But now Rafael saw her as a sort of any
time, any place and with any available man kind of girl.
He despised her and he wanted to humiliate her and he
had chosen the most machiavellian method possible. The
dark, primal depths of Rafael's essentially savage inner
self stood revealed, unleashed by anger and un-
quenchable arrogance. Why shouldn't he have what he
firmly believed she had given every other man she had
ever been with? She was the available space on his sexual
score-card, she reflected in disgust.

Four years ago, she had believed she knew
Rafael . . . but she hadn't known him at all. For a start,
she had accused him of being a sanctimonious stuffed
shirt that final night! Then, she hadn't known she was
being subjected to courtship Bolivian style, where you
received flowers, occasionally held hands, barely kissed
and generally conducted yourself with immense restraint
and maturity. But at just turned nineteen . . . I wanted
to dance all night in stuffy clubs, break speed limits in
the Ferrari, neck in the Ferrari, be seduced in the Ferrari,
drink pink champagne, wear outrageous attention-
grabbing clothes—his attention—be seen by all my
friends in a stretch limousine . . .

Glory be . . . She had been far less grown-up then than
she had fondly imagined. She only saw that now, looking
back, and frankly marvelled that Rafael could ever have
thought of marrying her. Had the wedding taken place,
there would probably be a gravestone out there somewhere by now, she thought, an almost hysterical giggle
lodged in her throat. She would have driven him crazy
by the end of the first six months!

The giggle died, her facial muscles tautening. But she
had loved him in the wild, head over heels, obsessive

style of her strong emotions. And, had he married her, she would no doubt have tried very hard to live up to his high standards... and with every failure she would have lost a little more courage. Rafael had a very powerful personality and a naturally domineering temperament. That came from being filthy rich and a lot brighter than ninety-nine per cent of the people around him. He would have swallowed her alive as a husband—only think of the traits he was freely demonstrating now...

Crazy... Yes, she had to be crazy, but she just couldn't help the thought that Rafael was a whole lot more exciting a prospect as a vengeful lover than he had ever been as an unnaturally courteous and yet despotic potential husband, striving to contain and control a naturally exuberant and rebellious teenager. They met as equals now, she told herself squarely—well, almost equals, she adjusted. He couldn't humiliate her unless she allowed him to do so. And he couldn't keep her here unless she chose to stay.

It was a kind of a compliment, she decided sleepily, that she should have left that strong an impression on a male of his experience. It was good to know that she hadn't been the only one burned that summer... but it was time he appreciated that, these days, Georgie was positively fireproof. A flame-thrower couldn't scorch her.

Only love could hurt—*love*. Her sultry mouth down-curved expressively. That prison of the mind which had made such a fool of her in the past? When she fell in love again, some day in the future, it would be with someone blond and blue-eyed and frightfully British, someone who fully appreciated her brains, her guts and her passion, and who thought he was one hell of a lucky guy to catch her. As she slid into sleep, at peace with herself at last, she smiled at that consoling image.

CHAPTER FIVE

GEORGIE made her plans while she was getting dressed the next morning. One way of another she needed to get off the *estancia* and persuading Rafael to do it for her would be the very easiest way to accomplish her escape. Deliciously sneaky, wonderfully simple. She strolled into the dining-room, vibrantly eye-catching in clinging pink Lycra shorts and an off-the-shoulder emerald lace-edged top. 'It's kind of quiet around here, isn't it?' she complained.

Rafael's brilliant dark eyes slowly swept over her. He lowered his newspaper, his expressive mouth twisting.

'Oh, no,' Georgie sighed mockingly. 'You don't like what I am wearing?'

'You are not on the beach,' Rafael responded drily.

'I have a thought for the day.' Georgie angled a brilliant smile at him. It wobbled slightly as she collided with piercing dark eyes, screened by lush ebony lashes, and her intended act slipped momentarily. He really was gorgeous—devastatingly, dangerously gorgeous. Had she married him and been able to tape his nasty mouth shut, she could probably have passed her time just looking at him and thinking utterly brainless thoughts of the 'he's mine' variety.

'Don't keep me in suspense,' he said with a distinctly cutting lack of interest.

Georgie tore a croissant to pieces with her restive hands, angry and dismayed by the sudden lurch of lost concentration evoked by her response to all that virile masculinity lounging at the other side of the polished table. 'Thank God, we *didn't* get married,' she said with helpless sincerity.

'You expect me to credit that you feel that way?' Rafael derided, arrogantly unimpressed.

'You'd have felt that way within two weeks if you had married me, and I bet there's never been a divorce in the family.' Georgie cast a speaking glance at the humourless dark faces of the portraits on the wall. 'Your ancestors were a pretty miserable bunch, weren't they? The men probably got rid of undesirable wives with childbirth. In those days, pregnancy was as dangerous as sky-diving. Poison was quite a common method too, or a fall down the stairs. In the Dark Ages, being a woman was being a victim. You could be beaten to death by your husband and nobody did a thing.'

Rafael murmured in a slightly strained tone, '*Desde luego*...of course, you were always fascinated by history. But to my knowledge none of my ancestors ever became that desperate.' He spread fluid hands and, without warning, his spontaneous laughter rang out, banishing the austerity from his dark features. 'Then, no doubt they took such dark secrets to their graves with them and, sadly, no one had the good sense to leave a diary of confession behind!'

Georgie was furious with herself for straying off stupidly into actual conversation with him and, worst of all, making him laugh. For a split-second, she absorbed his blatant amusement, and never before had she been more disturbingly aware of the intense charisma he possessed. Her face tightened. Hurriedly, she dived into the first move of her plan.

'Do we have to stay here?' she pressed abruptly.

His laughter died away, his eyes narrowing. 'I don't think I understand.'

She leant forward confidingly. 'I would be a whole lot more amenable—if you know what I mean—somewhere where I could have a little fun,' she told him softly, damning the tide of pink rising below her skin, terrified it would betray her. 'Twelve more hours out here in the boonies and I will drop dead with boredom. There is nothing but grass, cows and peasants out there.'

Inwardly, Georgie winced at the ignorant role she had chosen to play.

'My people are not peasants,' Rafael retorted with a flash of even white teeth, faint red darkening his hard cheekbones.

Georgie shrugged and thrust her chin back up again with determination, ready to play out her plan to the bitter end. 'Let's just put our cards on the table. You want me, you can have me, but there are certain—er—terms.'

'I want you, I can have you?' Intense golden eyes whipped over her beautiful face, resting on her hot cheeks. '*Now*, then . . . let us go upstairs,' he challenged smoothly.

Georgie's sip of coffee went down the wrong way. She coughed painfully, struggling to appear cool. 'Terms,' she reminded him chokily.

'Am I to understand this is a form of negotiation?' Rafael enquired with immense calm, lounging back in his carved chair to study her, very much as though she was the hired entertainment. 'Would you mind telling me what I am to receive in return?'

'You know damned fine what I'm offering you!' Georgie snapped back.

A beautifully shaped ebony brow elevated. 'What I could have had for nothing last night,' he prompted very softly.

Her teeth gnashed together, violence shimmering in her outraged violet eyes.

But, as she parted her lips, Rafael moved a silencing hand. He watched her with intense stillness. 'How amenable is amenable?' he encouraged lazily.

Hooked, she thought in triumph. 'Anything you want...whenever you want,' she whispered throatily, but she had to study the table to say it.

'And my side of the deal? Taking you somewhere without cattle and peasants?'

'I just want to have a good time and I'm not going to have it here, am I?' she pointed out tautly.

'Anything I want, whenever I want,' Rafael mused smoothly. 'But I have everything that I want right here. No deal.'

She stole a glance at his starkly handsome features, the cool dispassionate expression which revealed nothing. 'No deal?' she queried.

'Next time you try to bargain with me, be sure to arm yourself with the promise of something which isn't already mine for the taking.' Diamond-bright dark eyes raked over her furious face. 'For you are mine. And next time—and I hope there is a next time, for this has been the most entertaining breakfast I have had in years,' he confessed lethally, 'struggle not to look as if you're overdosing on cyanide when you're offering to be my sex-slave!'

'I am not yours and I never will be!' Georgie asserted fiercely. 'And I haven't got the temperament to be anybody's sex-slave!'

'But mine—and that awareness is killing you, isn't it?' Rafael traded lazily. 'You can screw around with all the men you like, but why not with me? What makes me different? Shall I tell you why you fight me to the best of your limited ability?'

A chill was enclosing her flesh. Another game had come to an end. She wanted to cover her ears and run but she sat there, looking blankly back at him, forcing herself not to reveal how sick she felt inside.

'You remember what it was like between us four years ago, before it started coming apart... and, deep down inside, you would very much like to have that romantic illusion back.'

She tasted blood in her mouth as her teeth bit into the soft underside of her lower lip. 'I wish I'd never met you, I certainly don't wish to relive any of it!'

'But the past is still there. You can't escape it... any more easily than you can escape me. In the thirty years of my life, I have been the focus of female seduction routines more times than I can count,' Rafael told her with harsh amusement. 'Women who know what they're doing. You don't appear to——'

'I'm not really interested in your opinion.'

'Subtlety evidently doesn't come with maturity. A Mae West impression at this hour of the day could only make me laugh.' Rafael expelled his breath audibly, shooting her a forbidding look from hooded dark eyes. 'Then you always did make me laugh, *es verdad*? It was that streak of highly deceptive naïveté which blinded me for so long to your real nature. I should have been warned by the birth-control pills I saw in your bag——'

'The *what*?' Georgie broke in with a furrowed brow, and then she tensed with comprehension.

Rafael shot her a sardonic glance. 'I assumed they were for my benefit.'

'You would.' Embarrassment held her only briefly.

'It should have occurred to me that you had already been involved in a sexual relationship, but then, my romanticised view of you did not allow such reasoning at that early stage.'

A ragged little laugh, empty of humour, fell from her strained mouth. Rafael was so sharp he would cut himself some day, and wasn't it fascinating to learn that he had been ready to misjudge her right from the beginning? Such a tiny thing, an oversight, a glimpse of a packet of pills in her bag, from which he had drawn incorrect conclusions. She would have died sooner than admit that she had been put on the contraceptive pill to regulate irregular periods.

She stood up. 'I think I need some fresh air,' she said jerkily.

'Georgie... strange as it may seem, I do not hold you responsible for a liaison begun at so early an age. You were the innocent party,' Rafael drawled with grave emphasis, his hard jawline clenching. 'But, at the time, I found the discovery of that particular relationship deeply offensive. It contravened my every principle of family-life, though I knew he was not in fact your brother——'

'What the heck are you talking about?'

'Did you think I didn't know?' Rafael threw back his imperious dark head, his challenging gaze imprisoning hers by blatant force of will.

'Didn't know what?' Tension had sprung into the atmosphere, thickening it. Georgie suddenly felt cold and threatened.

'Is the habit of secrecy still so engrained that you cannot be honest even after all this time?' Rafael demanded with derision. '*Por Dios* ... you live with him!'

Georgie went white by slow, painful degrees. Her tongue stole out to wet her dry lips. She could not believe that he would dare to suggest that she actually *lived* in the sexual sense with Steve or, indeed, that she had ever had an intimate relationship of any form with her stepbrother.

'I know,' Rafael repeated very quietly. 'I know that you began sharing his bed when you were seventeen.'

Her stomach curdled at the enormity of such a belief. 'That is the most disgusting thing anyone has ever accused me of,' she whispered strickenly, her distressed eyes clinging helplessly to his. 'And you can't believe it...you can't possibly believe it.'

Rafael rose fluidly upright, his hard golden features fiercely set. 'I prefer to have this out in the open between us. While I can appreciate your reluctance to face the fact that that liaison is no secret to me, I will *not* allow you to lie to me.'

He believed it. He actually believed that she had slept with Steve before she had even met *him*. Incredulous at the revelation, Georgie stared at him with wide, shocked eyes. 'You're crazy...absolutely crazy!'

Rafael stood back several feet from her, six feet two inches of darkly powerful masculinity. But, despite that distance, he had her cornered. Implacably obdurate dark eyes were trained on her. 'I am aware that my sister has no idea of that relationship, but surely your father and your stepmother cannot still be in the dark? Or are you telling me that it is now at an end and you remain just good friends under the same roof?' he derided.

'Steve doesn't even live under the same roof,' Georgie heard herself protest, her brain in too much turmoil for her to know where to attack first. 'He has an apartment now. He rents out the house to students at the college nearby. I have a tiny flat in the attic and I act as a sort of caretaker, keeping an eye on things...' Her voice simply drained away then as she wondered numbly why she was rabbiting on about something so utterly trivial.

'So it is over now——'

'It never began!' Georgie threw back with sudden wildness, her distress growing as the full connotations of what Rafael believed her capable of sank in. 'I've never had any sort of intimate relationship with Steve and I don't know how you can accuse me of something so disgusting! I've always thought of him as my brother——'

'That is all he ever should have been until you were old enough to know what you were doing. He took advantage of your youth and your passion, but you should have known that it was wrong,' Rafael delivered in harsh condemnation.

'You're not listening to me... are you? You don't believe me,' Georgie registered sickly.

Rafael vented a roughened laugh. 'I followed you home with him that last night. I didn't trust him with you. *Madre de Dios*... I didn't want to distress you with my suspicions about the exact nature of his feelings for you! Then, through the window, I saw you in his arms, lovers kissing passionately. Everything fell into place then. At last I understood.'

'You saw Steve kissing me?' Georgie echoed hollowly. 'But how...? The curtains weren't pulled,' she recalled abstractedly.

'Correct. I had a superb view...'

Georgie was deep in shock. Rafael had opened a locked door on the past, filling in details she hadn't been aware of then. But he had twisted the picture as she knew it and flung her into violent turmoil. 'It wasn't what you thought,' she burst out abruptly.

'The only acceptable response now is the whole truth and nothing but the truth!' Rafael delivered with murderous quietness. 'And I do believe I'm entitled to ask one question.'

Numbly she looked back at him, pale and shaken and unbearably tense.

'While you were seeing me, were you *still* sleeping with him?'

'Dear God...' Georgie was so appalled that her stomach responded with a nauseous lurch of protest.

'So you weren't. One small consolation,' Rafael breathed scathingly. 'Then I supplanted him. Were I generous, I should now excuse his every jealous attempt to come between us, but I excuse nothing that he did and I blame you for deliberately deceiving me into believing that you were innocent. Did it amuse you? Or did you want to believe that you could carry the deception through to the bitter end?'

Georgie covered her face with her hands and turned unsteadily away, desperate to escape that lethal accented drawl.

'I believed you would marry him,' Rafael admitted harshly. 'For years, I have expected to hear news of your marriage through my sister. Instead, what do I hear? One man after another—*friends*, María Cristina trustingly calls them—but you and I both know that you lie back on the nearest bed for your male "friends"...'

Suddenly Georgie just couldn't take any more, and the very abruptness with which she dived past him took him by surprise. She flew out of the house, running without even knowing where she was going. Her heart was thumping sickly in her throat, every sobbing intake of oxygen rattling through her lungs. She wanted to take off like a jet plane and leave everything that distressed her far behind, but the torment of pain was remorselessly trapped inside her and she was stuck with it.

The heat swiftly sapped her energy. She got a stitch in her side and had to stop and bend over, struggling to get her breath back, the dusty ground below her feet tilting sickeningly up at her.

'Georgie!'

Her head whirled up. She saw Rafael moving with long, determined strides towards her and panic filled her. No more. Right now, she really couldn't take any more! Her fevered eyes whirled round the cluster of buildings near and far, passing blindly over the curious faces of the people in the vicinity, and then she saw the pretty little whitewashed church with its open doors and took off again.

The coolness of the dim interior engulfed her in welcome. Her feet took her down the aisle into a seat in the shadow of a stone pillar. Wrapping her arms round herself, she attempted to catch her breath and banish the awful nausea threatening. Shock. She knew what was wrong with her. Shock and a kind of horrified disbelief that even Rafael could believe such things of her.

'This is not the place for you,' Rafael murmured in a stifled undertone from behind her.

'Go away,' she mumbled. Did he think she was going to desecrate his precious church by her mere presence? She wouldn't be surprised if he did. And even in the Middle Ages, Rafael wouldn't have allowed her sanctuary here. He would have dragged her out and thrown her to the crowd to be torn apart, no doubt, she reflected wildly. Rafael was a savage and, with anyone who fell into the whore category, he was a throwback to the Spanish Inquisition.

And then she heard another voice—very quiet, very calm—speak in Spanish, and there was one of those explosive silences which could be physically felt... It seemed to go on forever and ever before she heard the astonishing but unmistakable sound of Rafael's retreat. Only then did she appreciate that for once impulse had not betrayed her. The church was the one place Rafael Rodriguez Berganza did not rule supreme.

She knew her saviour had to have been the priest, and she waited shakily to be forced into speech, but no voice spoke and the silence stayed, slowly soothing the tumult of her emotional upheaval, enabling her to think again.

So now she knew why Rafael had refused to listen to her attempts to explain the platonic nature of her friendship with Danny. He had been suspicious of her morals long before that day. The pills—then what? Steve's dislike of him? Steve had not been jealous, for goodness' sake! Steve simply hadn't liked Rafael. And when Rafael had seen that embrace, he had forced every other fact to fit, choosing to assume that that accidental glimpse was merely the tip of the iceberg in a far more intimate relationship. After all, hadn't she been shamelessly encouraging towards him?

Had her passionate response to him been that misleading? Had she come across as some sort of nymphomaniac? He had a wild imagination... Or had he? Witnessing that embrace certainly would have been a shock, as much of a shock for Rafael as it had been at the time for Georgie. Rafael could never have seen a hint of such intimacy in her behaviour with Steve at any other time. And that fact alone might well have been the final confirmation of Rafael's suspicions. Clearly he had believed that she and Steve were polished pretenders at being simply stepbrother and sister in public view, an act they had put on to conceal their true relationship from family and friends.

Moisture dripped on her tightly clenched hands. She lifted an uncertain hand to her damp face, discovered she was crying. It was so very hard to try and be calm about an accusation so outrageous and so distressing. But that same accusation revealed so much about Rafael. She shuddered.

From the outset Rafael had been sickly prejudiced against her. He had probably fought hard against the attraction between them and, even in succumbing to that attraction, he had still been on red alert for any flaws that she might display. Desire had driven Rafael, and the price of fulfilling that desire had been marriage.

But intellectually, of course, he *hadn't* wanted to marry her. If it hadn't been for her connection with María Cristina, Rafael would just have taken what was on offer and slept with her, slaking his desire in the most basic way possible. Subconsciously, he must have fiercely resented that reality. So it must have been relatively easy for Rafael to begin to suspect that her innocence was an act, and fate had been wonderfully kind to him in serving up the kind of evidence he required to convince himself that she was a whore instead.

Rafael had run true to type, she reflected numbly. Hot-blooded, suspicious, jealous and melodramatic—the archetypal smouldering Latin lover. Yet it was so difficult to equate that image with the freezingly self-contained male who had rejected her at their final meeting. He had not mentioned Steve then. Why not? Had it been beneath his precious dignity to reveal the extent to which he believed himself to have been deceived? He had not called her a whore, either. Indeed, in retrospect, she realised that Rafael had been remarkably restrained that day. But it was almost laughable that he could have believed her steeped in sexual sin at so tender an age. But she couldn't laugh, had never felt further from laughter.

She felt agonisingly hurt and bitter and it was that incredible pain which she now feared most of all. Her pride and her principles revolted against the image Rafael now had of her. Yes, perhaps she would have liked the romantic illusion back, just as he had shrewdly divined. Being treated like a scarlet woman might have briefly appealed to her sense of humour when she put on an act that first night in an effort to hold her own, but with Rafael, she could never ever forget that once she had loved him.

The memory was just there in the back of her mind all the time, warning her that she was vulnerable, warning her that she still found him staggeringly attractive on a purely physical level, and that something inside her which she was deeply ashamed of made her behave more outrageously around him than she would ever have dreamt of behaving around any other man. Why was that? Was there actually a part of her which rejoiced in his desire for her body? Could she be that stupid? Hurriedly, she rose from the worn wooden pew.

She was walking towards the blinding sunlight flooding through the doors when the portly little priest appeared before her. 'I am Father Tomás Garcia,' he told her in perfect English, extending a polite hand that couldn't be ignored. 'And you are Georgie, María Cristina's friend.'

Taken aback by the assurance with which that statement was made, Georgie mumbled she knew not what.

'Would you like some tea? Or possibly some lemonade? This is the hottest part of the day and I think you must be very thirsty. You are a teacher, aren't you? A fine profession, but more challenging now than it was in my time,' he remarked, accompanying her outside and turning towards the small house in the shadow of the church. 'Primary or secondary level?' he prompted with interest.

Ten minutes later, Georgie was ensconced in a comfortable armchair with a glass of lemonade, in a cluttered but sparsely furnished sitting-room, and she didn't quite know how she had got there. 'You know,' she muttered uneasily, fearing that the little priest was acting on a false assumption, 'I'm C of E.'

Father Garcia chuckled. 'I'll forgive you. You were telling me about your history course,' he reminded her.

It was over an hour before she departed, and her throat ought to have been sore from talking so much. After all, when all her years at college had been exhausted, they had somehow moved on to her family and from there to London, which her companion had visited forty years earlier and never forgotten. She was astonished by how relaxed she felt as she turned uncertainly back.

'Thanks,' she said huskily.

'For what do you thank me?' Father Garcia's sparkling brown eyes, so lively in his round, peaceful face, rested on her intently. 'It has been a very great pleasure for me to make the acquaintance of Rafael's bride-to-be.'

'*Bride*?' Georgie couldn't help it; the repetition erupted helplessly from her startled lips and even to her own ears she sounded like a cat whose tail had been trodden on.

'Fiancée?' the little priest suggested with apparently unshakeable good humour that took no note of her shock. 'That is the modern term, I suppose.'

'I'm afraid you've misunderstood,' Georgie began, in an agony of discomfiture.

'It is supposed to be a secret? But how could it be *here*?' Father Garcia's expressive eyes twinkled merrily. 'Naturally we are all excited at the prospect of Rafael's marriage.'

And off he went before Georgie could unglue her tongue from the roof of her dry mouth. Dear heaven, did Rafael have any idea of the expectations he had raised by bringing her here? Father Garcia had spoken of their marriage as though it was one centimetre short of accomplished fact, and she had only arrived yesterday! Was he aware that Rafael had once planned to marry her?

In a renewed state of turmoil, Georgie headed back to the house, but this time she was abnormally conscious of the number of smiles and inquisitive looks she received on the way. Without hesitation she went off in search of Rafael, determined to demand transport off the *estancia* again. This farce had gone far enough! He simply couldn't keep her here against her wishes!

He was on the phone in the library, which he appeared to use as an office. As she burst through the door his gleaming dark head jerked round, an expression of astonishment briefly etched on his devastatingly handsome features. Presumably nobody ever entered the inner sanctum without a knock and official permission.

'I will be with you in a moment.' It was a cool aside.

Stalking over to the window, Georgie turned her back on him and jerkily folded her arms. She listened to him talk in fast, idiomatic French, his accent and inflexion flawless. It set her teeth on edge. He was rapping out orders like the feudal autocrat that he was. When the call was concluded, she spun round.

'I hear that Father Tomás has been entertaining you——'

'The grapevine is supersonic around here, isn't it?' Georgie cut in, throwing her vibrant head back and watching him with a bright little smile pinned to her sultry mouth. 'Did your little bird also tell you that he thinks we're about to get married?'

'What an extraordinary idea,' Rafael gibed without pause, betraying not an ounce of the discomfiture she had expected to rouse. Eyes dark as Hades raked over her and his sensual mouth twisted wtih cruel amusement. 'I may have gone overboard in my lust to possess you four years ago, but you will recall that I didn't ever get as far as a proposal. In short, *querida*, men like me don't marry women like you, unless they are suffering from temporary insanity.'

The angry flush on her beautiful face slowly receded, leaving her painfully drawn.

'You see,' Rafael extended indolently, 'I first met you at a time when I was bored with the easy availability of your sex. No woman was ever a challenge. Every woman I ever wanted came to me, shared my bed, did whatever it took to try and hold my attention. I wanted to be the hunter but I never needed to exert myself——'

'I don't want to hear this!' Georgie interrupted with sudden violence.

'I want you to hear it.' Rafael lounged gracefully up against his solid antique desk and surveyed her with hooded dark eyes. 'And then, one day, I met quite unexpectedly the most stunningly beautiful girl, who blushed with enchanting regularity and looked at me with what seemed to be her every thought written in her gorgeous eyes. But this stunningly beautiful girl was untouchable by virtue of her youth. And that for me was the very essence of the romance which every other woman had been so quick in her eagerness to deny me. Don't look so staggered...remember, I was only twenty-four,' he reminded her with sardonic bite. 'And, with hindsight, not one half as clever as I liked to think I was!'

'Don't!' Georgie was disturbed by his savage self-mockery, and her nails dug painfully into her palms.

'Men always want what is out of reach. That was three-quarters of your attraction,' Rafael asserted drily. 'And as I got to know you—or believed I was getting to know you—I also discovered that you were bright, amusing and apparently outspokenly honest, a trait which for me was on a par with your beauty. Having to wait for you undoubtedly increased your desirability tenfold. I had never had to wait for anything in my life before and, while I waited, I endowed you with every conceivable virtue.'

The contempt with which he cynically dismissed what he had felt then angered and hurt Georgie. He resurrected memories of those innocent days and those memories burnt her now like acid. 'I don't believe in looking back,' she said tautly. 'It's a mistake.'

Rafael spread long brown fingers in a gesture of careless disagreement. 'I'm not so sensitive,' he drawled. 'You were a learning experience for me. Different culture, different values. I was young enough to believe that things like that didn't matter...but they do, very much.'

'Why on earth did you bring me here?' Georgie demanded shakily, denying the creeping tide of mortification consuming her.

'An overwhelming desire to punish you, and so far, I have to confess, it has been an extraordinarily satisfying experience,' Rafael murmured without remorse.

'You swine...you utter swine,' Georgie whispered in a stricken rush.

A slanting ebony brow quirked. 'But not yet quite as satisfying as I anticipate. I want you lying under me, gasping with excitement, begging for release. And after I have had you, I will be entirely satisfied. Playing this waiting game merely adds an edge.'

Without even thinking about it, Georgie hit him, the crack of her palm resoundingly loud in the smouldering silence. He didn't even flinch. The reddened mark of her fingers darkened one savage cheekbone. He snaked out a powerful arm and yanked her between his spread thighs, reading the raw apprehension flaring in her wide eyes. Incandescent gold raked over her scared face and abruptly he laughed. 'I'll take it out of your hide in bed. That's a first, Georgie. No woman has ever struck me before.'

'I hate you!' Georgie launched, with a sob of distress snatching at her raw vocal cords. 'I don't know how you can do this to me!'

'So easily, it would terrify you,' Rafael shared almost conversationally. 'In fact, I could develop quite a taste for your tears. Poor Georgie, one last dangerous impulse backed you into the tightest corner of all!' Long fingers forced up her chin, quelling her attempt to evade him. 'So impetuous, so uncontrolled...so very different from me. I was raised to be intensely disciplined, responsible, serious——'

'I'm not interested!' she spat back at him, appalled by his insight into her character. 'Let go!'

'And you panic with such naked abandon,' he murmured flatly. 'I was a bastard after breakfast, wasn't I? But then I wanted the truth——'

'But it wasn't the truth! It was what you wanted to believe!' Georgie condemned hotly. 'What you'd like to believe so that you can excuse yourself for treating me like dirt!'

Rafael laced a hard hand into her tumbling hair and tightened his fingers with painful thoroughness. 'He was your lover. I know it and, before I'm finished with you, you'll admit it,' he swore.

'For heaven's sake, I've never had a lover!' Georgie slung back at him between gritted teeth. 'And I'm sick to death of you acting like I'm some sort of raving nymphomaniac!'

'You've never had a lover?' Glittering dark eyes raked hers with pitying derision. 'Georgie... do you think I believe in those mermaids upstairs?' he asked very drily. 'Why pretend? It doesn't matter any more. But lies infuriate me.'

It was useless. She saw that and regretted her honesty. 'Please let go of me,' she muttered.

Astonishingly, he released her and Georgie backed away on cottonwool legs, trembling in spite of her efforts to control that physical weakness.

'You are ashamed of your relationship with him now,' Rafael breathed with smouldering dark golden eyes pinned contemptuously to her. 'A little too late to impress.'

'Go to hell!' she spat, her throat choked up with tears. 'I detest you!'

'But it's the wanting that hurts most, *es verdad*?' Rafael dealt her a slashing look of cruelly amused comprehension.

'I'd sooner go to bed with a—with a total stranger!'

'Oh, I'm sure you've done that at least once,' Rafael drawled with laconic certainty. 'Exclusive, you're not.'

Outraged, Georgie stalked back to him. 'Well, then, you're not very fastidious, are you?' she hissed, in a tone shaking with red-hot fury and frustration at her inability to shut him up. 'But brace yourself for disappointment, Rafael. After this morning's little honesty session, I would be certifiably insane to let you anywhere near me.'

He reached for her and she bristled like a spitting cat, ready to claw as she went into startled retreat, registering her mistaken direction only as the wall connected with her taut shoulderblades. 'I will not stand for this!' she erupted in a burst of indignation.

As Rafael closed the distance between them, an appreciative smile slashed his golden features. 'You are so much more entertaining now than you were then. Four years ago, it was, "Yes, Rafael, no, Rafael, whatever you think, Rafael," and I couldn't understand where all your spirit had gone,' he confided, bracing a hand on either side of her head. 'Of course, it was an act put on to impress. Then you were playing for high stakes. You may not have guessed what was on my mind but your goal was certainly marriage——'

'Like hell it was!' Incensed by the scathing accusation, Georgie's every muscle clenched defensively as he deliberately moved closer. 'Now, back off!'

'But that is not what you want.' Rafael lowered his dark head, veiled eyes a shimmer of hot gold on her wildly flushed face, and she was entrapped by a curious stillness, her breath locked in her constricted throat. 'What you want with every fibre of your being is to possess me as thoroughly as I intend to possess you...'

CHAPTER SIX

GEORGIE was mesmerised by the savage brilliance of Rafael's sexually explicit gaze and the ragged edge of blatant need in his dark, deep voice. The familiar musky scent of him teased at her flaring nostrils as he dropped a hand to her hip and suddenly hauled her against him. Her heart raced crazily. The hard thrust of his masculine arousal pulsed against her abdomen and then he lifted her up to him with a powerful ease that exhilarated her. For a split-second she was looking down at him and hunger tore at her with cruel claws, ripping away every proud layer of pretence.

A desperate pain pierced her then, a terrible vulnerability. In all this time, all these years, no other man had ever drawn her as he did. In the dark of the night, in the secrecy of her dreams, she had tossed and turned and craved him, and despised herself for that treacherous yearning. But now, as she clashed with devouring golden eyes and burned, she felt the answering tremor of response snaking through his magnificent physique.

His arms tightened fiercely around her and he drew her down, taking her mouth in a deep, shuddering admission of need that sent her every sense rocketing to fever-pitch. And she knew then that the power was not his alone. Wrapped round him like a vine, Georgie kissed him back with all the fire he had awakened. As his tongue penetrated between her parted lips, her nails dug into his broad shoulders, a stifled whimper of excitement escaping her.

97

Rafael groaned something in his own language and swept her right off her feet with bruisingly impatient hands. She captured his hard cheekbones between her palms and stared up at him with dazed eyes, out of focus with passion. He succumbed to the lure of her swollen mouth again somewhere halfway up the stairs and control seemed to go out of the window at that point, because he braced her against the wall and took her lips with a driving, demanding sexuality which reduced her to mental rubble.

'*Madre de Dios...*' he swore roughly against her throat, struggling for breath, and then he carried her up into the bedroom, tumbled her down on the bed and pinned her there with a wildly exciting lack of cool.

He wrenched his jacket and tie off and ripped at his shirt without breaking the connection of their mouths once. Her heartbeat thundered in her ears like a pulsebeat of desire. His fingers found the neckline of her cotton top and tore it down over her arms. He curved his hands over the shameless thrust of her pouting breasts and she shivered in violent reaction, helplessly arching her back to increase the pressure on her unbearably sensitive nipples.

He seized on a taut rosy crest with his teeth and the explosion of sensation he released made her cry out, her teeth gritting, her throat extending.

'*Perdición*' he groaned, lifting his arrogant dark head to look down at her as he dealt at speed with the remainder of his clothing. 'So long... I have waited so long for this.'

So long, yes, she thought intensely, reaching back up for him with the single-minded motivation of a programmed doll. A relentless hunger seized her as he sealed his virile length to hers. Her whole body flushed with consuming heat and she turned to him, driven by something much more powerful than she was, and let her hands travel through the light mat of curling black hair across his muscular chest, glorying in the freedom to touch him at last.

Raising his head, he pressed her down to the pillows again, stilling her fluttering hands, the dominant male, sentencing her back to passivity. From below ebony lashes he dealt her a wholly predatory look that made her burn and quiver. He reached down and peeled off her shorts and panties in one impatient movement. He thrust a hair-roughened thigh between hers and fanned out her hair with his fingers so that the vibrant strands surrounded her exquisite face, tumbling in a fiery cascade across the white pillows. From somewhere he had found control again and now he contemplated her with an indolent air of possession.

Georgie trembled and met that look and suddenly remembered about *this* bed, *this* room. The significance of their surroundings and the recollection of his savage desire for revenge suddenly chilled her to the marrow. 'No,' she said shakily. 'Not here——'

'*Sí* . . . it is what I want,' Rafael said softly.

'But not what I want!' Georgie suddenly gasped, the ability to think returning by degrees in dangerous little warning spurts.

'All you want is me.' Rafael evaded her attempt to drag herself free of his intimate hold and flattened her back to the mattress with his vastly superior strength. He subjected her to a wolfish appraisal, golden hawk eyes scanning her shocked and confused face with a devastatingly cruel amusement. 'Your one virtue. All you ever wanted was me from the very first moment. It wasn't the limo, it wasn't the accent and it wasn't any schoolgirl fantasy either,' he asserted. 'It was far more basic. An intense sexual desire to possess and be possessed.'

'No.' Georgie sucked in air and shook her head back and forth in urgent negative.

His thumb pried apart her lips, brushed against her teeth. 'And you can't control it...unnerving, isn't it?'

The tip of her tongue brushed of its own volition against his thumb and then withdrew sharply as he laughed. 'Is it?' she whispered.

'You tell me... Here, now, you're *mine* to do with exactly as I please.' To illustrate that raw assurance, Rafael bent his head and circled a distended pink nipple with his tongue and then his teeth, and the entire conversation was, for Georgie, plunged into some dark limbo as her swollen sensitive flesh screamed with sensation and craved more.

He took her mouth with carnal expertise, slowly, tormentingly, denying her the greater force that her every skin-cell demanded, until her hands rose and speared into his hair and she held him to her, quivering with unabated need, surrendering to the incredibly powerful urges of her own body.

His fingers roamed over her flat, taut stomach and into the damp tangle of curls at the apex of her thighs and suddenly she couldn't be still any more, suddenly she was burning alive. He explored the moist tender flesh with a knowing eroticism that made her breath sob in her throat. Nothing could have prepared her for the intensity of the pleasure or the electrifying throb of primal excitement making her hips rise in supplication. There was an ache now, an intolerable ache, building down deep inside her.

'*Cristo* ... you're so tight.'

She heard him groan, but no words could connect now. Her brain had shut down. Every response she gave was instinctive and out of control. She writhed as he cupped her hips and came down on her, was suddenly stilled by forceful hands, and then she felt him, the hot thrusting hardness of his masculinity alien against her. Her eyes flew wide with an intuitive fear of the unknown and she met the pagan stamp of intense desire on his dark features above hers. Another kind of ache stirred inside her, tugging violently at her heartstrings, making her lie back in helpless submission, trembling with the force of her own need.

'*Dios*...you feel like a virgin.'

His hand pushed her thighs wider, higher, drawing her up to receive him. He entered her with one sure thrust and the piercing pain of his intrusion took her completely by surprise.

'Georgie...' Golden eyes abruptly swept hers, a frown of incomprehension drawing his arrow-straight ebony brows together. '*No...imposible*,' he groaned, black lashes dropping low on his damp, driven features as he moved again in an instinctive surge to deepen his possession.

Her teeth sank stoically into the soft underside of her lower lip, for beyond the pain was the most extraordinary pleasure at the feel of him inside her. Intimate beyond belief. Heat flooded her in a blinding wave. She could feel the force of the control he was exerting as he thrust slowly, carefully into the very heart of her. His breathing was ragged, his sweat-slicked body sliding against her supersensitive flesh, and she threw her head back, moaning his name as the pressure began to build again unbearably.

Every new sensation was torturously intense. Her heart slammed madly against her ribcage as he began to drive into her faster, harder, with shredding control and fierce, masculine domination. The pleasure took her over, rising to a shattering crescendo that plunged her entire body into quivering, indescribable ecstasy. Above her, she felt him reach the same plateau and shudder and groan as he sank deep into her one last time.

Afterwards she was in a state of prolonged shock, still lost in the intensity of extraordinary physical response.

He lay in the circle of her arms and she liked that so much, the weight of him, the feel of him, the so familiar scent of him that when he shifted away she felt disturbingly bereft as he flopped down on the pillows beside her in the thrumming silence. Her fingers curled into fists by her sides until she conquered the terrible urge to reach back for him, for that closeness her every sense craved.

Was she crazy? a little voice asked. They were not lovers in any sense of the word. There was no relationship, no tenderness, no love. Suddenly she felt empty and cold. But everyone had the right to sin at least once in a lifetime, didn't they? And Rafael was *her* sin. Just this one time and never again. They had made love—no, they had had sex, she adjusted, her troubled face tightening as she fought off a dismaying sense of vulnerability. He had not used her any more than she had used him, she told herself fiercely. She had always wanted Rafael Rodriguez Berganza...

'I'll buy you an apartment in Paris,' Rafael murmured smoothly into the silence. 'There will be times you will be able to travel with me... if you can be discreet, but you will never be able to come here again and you will have to break off your correspondence with my sister. You will live like a princess. I will give you everything but my name.'

It was like having a knife driven into her heart. Her stomach twisted sickly. He was so unemotional. Was this what she had waited for all these years? An invitation to be his mistress? A shudder of revulsion assailed her. So he didn't use you any more than you used him? Who are you kidding, Georgie? You are not up to this, you are way out of your depth.

'Say something... anything.' Rafael leant over her without warning and skimmed a surprisingly unsteady hand over the damp tendrils of hair clinging to her brow.

The nagging ache between her thighs felt like the greatest act of treachery she could ever have committed against herself. She clashed one fleeting time with brilliant dark eyes scanning her with probing intent, and hurriedly looked away again, hating herself.

'*Madre de Dios*!' The interruption to her frantic thoughts of shame and self-reproach was explosive. 'Georgie——?'

'I need a bath,' she mumbled, not listening, still glued to the edge of the bed and struggling for the act of courage it was going to take to walk across the room naked as a jaybird. But escape was definitely a necessity.

A hand like an iron vice closed round her forearm and turned her back abruptly to face him. Rafael stared at her with fierce demand in his eyes. His rigid facial cast and the pallor below his naturally golden skin betrayed his state of shock.

'What's wrong?' she questioned.

'Tell me that doesn't mean what I think it does...' Rafael urged in a ragged undertone.

Her brow furrowed, Georgie followed the direction of his gaze and saw the bloodstain on the sheet. She was appalled. She wanted to cover it again. But it was too late. He had seen it. She just couldn't believe that her body could have let her down like that. A keen athlete from an early age, it had never occurred to her that there could possibly be any physical evidence of her lost innocence.

'You were untouched,' Rafael breathed, driving a set of long brown fingers roughly through his tousled hair.

'Don't be ridiculous!' Georgie scoffed, lifting a pillow to hug.

'Look at me.'

Her sultry mouth set in a positively vicious line of mutiny. His shaken voice told her he was on the edge of extinction by severe shock.

'You were a virgin——'

'Nonsense! Now, if you don't mind, I'd like this bed back to myself.'

Abruptly, he snatched the pillow off her and flattened her back to the mattress with two very forceful and determined hands. 'I mind...I mind very much.'

Shattered, Georgie's eyes collided with tormented dark ones that devoured her every fleeting expression. 'Will you stop looking at me like that?'

'I felt the barrier...I told myself I was crazy...I just couldn't believe it!' Rafael vented unsteadily.

'I don't know what you're talking about——'

'Stop it, Georgie,' Rafael grated rawly. 'You were a virgin!'

'Will you stop saying that?'

'Admit it.'

'OK—big deal, I don't think—you were the first, so go and notch your bloody bedpost!' Georgie shrieked back, a boiling tide of embarrassing moisture dammed up behind her eyelids.

'*Dios*...but how is it possible?' Rafael demanded with a groan.

'Just leave me alone!'

Without warning, he pulled her into his arms. She could feel the raw tension still sizzling through him. She was as rigid as a mannequin in his embrace. Seemingly impervious to that lack of encouragement, he released his breath in a hiss. 'Forgive me...can you ever forgive me for what I have done?' he muttered unevenly. 'But to make such a sacrifice to prove to me how wrong I have been... How can I ever make that up to you?'

Cursing the reality that Rafael always cornered her when she was least capable of self-defence, Georgie was attempting to fight through the absolute turmoil of her own confusion. But that final incredible statement pierced the tumult and froze her. Rafael actually believed that she had made him a gift of her inexperience simply to prove that he had been wrong about her promiscuity all along. It was the most nauseating suggestion Georgie had ever heard.

'Well, you don't need to make it up to me, because I wasn't trying to prove anything! Your opinion of me, Rafael, is absolutely immaterial to my peace of mind.'

'You cannot mean that,' Rafael said with flat disbelief.

Georgie fought out of his temporarily loosened hold and grabbed the sheet round her. 'I'm sorry, I do mean it. Such an idea never once occurred to me,' she snapped, thoroughly fed up that he just wouldn't take the hint and leave her alone with the tumultuous mess of emotion that was sloshing around inside her.

'Not *that*,' he stressed. 'You cannot mean that my opinion means nothing to you after what we have just shared.'

'Wasn't exactly a communion of souls, was it?' Georgie heard herself say snidely. 'We had sex——'

'We made love——'

'We screwed,' Georgie broke in, determined to have the last word.

'Don't talk like that!' Outraged golden eyes raked over her.

'Oh, is that one of those expressions which you're allowed to use and I'm not? Tough,' Georgie muttered tightly, pleating the sheet between her fingers, recognising that she was hopelessly engulfed in bitterness. 'I really can't understand why you're going on like this about something so trivial.'

Long fingers curved round her arms, dragging her round to face him. 'After all that has happened between us, how could it possibly be trivial?' he demanded savagely.

'Not many women go to the grave virgins. For heaven's sake, I'm twenty-three and I just thought it was time...

Well, to be honest, I didn't think at all,' Georgie adjusted with essential honesty. 'But if I had realised there was going to be a heavy post-mortem, I wouldn't have bothered, I can tell you that!'

'You're upset, embarrassed...I am spoiling everything,' he breathed starkly.

'You generally do when you open your mouth. I ought to be used to it by now.'

'My conscience...it is eating me alive,' he confessed tightly, reaching for one of her tightly clenched hands and smoothing out the small fingers. 'I have hurt you so much. You tried to defend yourself four years ago and I wouldn't listen to you. Why won't you look at me? Why won't you speak?'

'I'll probably be a bit more slick the next time I have a one-night stand,' Georgie bit out acidly, but she could hear the tremor in her own voice, the thickness of tears she was holding back. She snatched her hand back.

'There won't be a next time.'

No, he was right there. Nothing like learning the hard way, Georgie! Do you ever learn any other way? The last thing she needed was Rafael's guilt. It made her want to scream and claw at him. She had her pride, like anyone else, but it seemed to her that he was set on depriving her of even that. The past was past. She had no desire to reopen that particular Pandora's box.

Or the even more recent past. All that shameless rolling about and moaning she had done for his benefit—well, that was so far in the past that it was pre-civilisation as far as she was concerned. The worst mistake of her life. He treated her like dirt beneath his aristocratic feet and she rewarded him by falling into bed with him. A single tear rolled down her cheekbone, stinging her tender skin on its passage.

'*Querida*...please...please don't cry,' Rafael groaned. 'Anything you want, anything it takes, I will make it up to you...'

'A flight to La Paz.' Escape. That was all that was on Georgie's mind.

'That isn't what you really want,' Rafael assured her with harsh emphasis.

And that was the last straw. Georgie looked at him, her facial muscles stiff with pure rage. 'How the hell would you know what *I* want?'

He slung her a thwarted look, raw with a kind of incredulous frustration, and sprang off the bed to stride into the bathroom.

Georgie flopped back down again. 'Good riddance,' she muttered out loud.

Then she rolled over and buried her convulsing face furiously into the tumbled pillows. Why wouldn't he just leave her alone? Didn't he have his own bathroom? She reined the sobs back, wouldn't cry, wouldn't have cried if he'd held her upside-down over a bonfire and tortured her. Making an outsize fool of herself once in one day was enough.

This was the end of something that had started four years ago—no, six years ago, when she had first laid eyes on Rafael Rodriguez Berganza. A terrifying obsession which had grown out of a teenage infatuation. It was finished now. The act of sex had finished it forever. But what a shame it was that she had to sacrifice her friendship with María Cristina on the same funeral pyre.

For she would have no other choice. The last connection had to be severed. There would be no more letters bearing continuous little snippets of information about Rafael... Sometimes Rafael's sister had written so much about him that Georgie had wondered if her friend's own life was so empty that she had nothing better to write about. On the face of it, what possible interest could Georgie have been supposed to have in Rafael's travels, his speeches and his business interests, with never an indiscreet word about the women in his life?

But those letters, she appreciated, had kept Rafael alive inside her mind and her memory. Well, she needed to go on with her life and leave him behind her where he belonged, and she couldn't possibly do that and still stay in touch with María Cristina! Her throat thickened with renewed bitterness.

In the midst of her turmoil, Georgie was scooped without warning off the bed. 'What are you doing?'

'I ran a bath for you.'

'Why?' Georgie demanded baldly.

'Because it would appear to be about the only thing I can currently do that might be right,' Rafael delivered shortly, whipped off the sheet which had been wrapped round her and slid her into the warm water before she knew what was happening to her.

In silence, Georgie hugged her knees, dead centre of the splendid marble bath, her tumbled head downbent as she stared blindly down into the water.

'As God is my witness, I will kill him,' Rafael intoned with a murderous quietness that was somehow explosive in the charged silence.

'Kill who?' she mumbled without much interest, too caught up in her own stark sense of failure and inadequacy.

'Nobody important,' Rafael murmured smoothly.

'I want to go home,' she said tightly.

'I thought you wanted to see María Cristina and...and George.'

Astonishment held her taut and then drifted away again. Nothing like a rousing dose of guilt for the Latin conscience, she reflected. 'No.'

'*No*?' Rafael repeated, his disbelief at the careless denial palpable.

'No,' she said again.

'Why? No, forget I asked...' Rafael urged in abrupt retreat.

Later she didn't know how long she had sat there before she mechanically washed and then dried herself, and padded back to the bedroom. The sheet had been changed. Her cheeks burned. Marvellous, now everybody would know! Well, that was it. She wasn't budging out of this bedroom until he had that flight arranged! Donning a nightdress with shaking hands, Georgie got back into bed, great rolling breakers of misery submerging her.

Now—now, why didn't she bring it out and face it? Just when had she fallen in love with Rafael? Six years ago, four years ago or just yesterday? Did the timing really matter? He had turned away from her after slaking his lust. Then, she had suspected herself but, by the time he got around to suggesting the life of a kept woman in Paris, suspicion had become painful fact. That had been the final humiliation. To love a man who had caused her this much pain was insanity.

Pride, self-interest and intelligence ruled against loving a complete bastard. But the fact of the matter was that she *did* love him, could still hate him with unvarnished energy and passion when he hurt or angered her, but underneath all that was the love and this truly paralysing longing to be loved back. It terrified her. What had he ever done to be worthy of her love? Nothing, not a single damned thing!

She fell asleep and was wakened by a tiny sound. Startled, she sat up, saw Rafael standing over her and visibly flinched, her natural colour draining away.

'I brought you up some dinner... you were asleep at lunchtime,' he proffered tautly.

Georgie was stunned. Rafael with a tray. As unnatural a sight as Rafael up to his elbows in a sink full of dishes.

He looked a little rough too, a blue shadow darkening his strong jawline, harsh lines of strain between his arrogant nose and hard mouth. His tie was loose at his brown throat, a couple of buttons on his shirt undone, revealing a whorl of black, curling hair.

She dragged her uncertain eyes from him. 'Thanks,' she said woodenly.

He strolled round to the foot of the brass bed and closed his brown hands round the top rail. 'I explained to Teresa that you had been taken ill... and——' he hesitated '—I changed the bed,' he added in a strained undertone.

He had changed the bed. What the heck was going on here? Why was he behaving in this weird way? She was willing to bet that Rafael had never changed a bed in his life before. Of course, he was hiding the evidence. She suddenly wished she were a corpse. Now, that would have given him a real challenge to get his teeth into, the sort of challenge he really deserved. She just bet she was on a flight home tomorrow.

'We need to talk,' he drawled, when it became painfully obvious that Georgie was not about to break the silence.

'No.' She didn't even lift her head.

'Then I will talk and you will listen.'

'You could have nothing to say that I could possibly want to hear.'

A lean hand abruptly slashed through the air in a raking gesture of raw impatience. 'I make no excuses for my behaviour over the past forty-eight hours. I must have been out of my mind,' he admitted in a driven undertone. 'I abandoned every principle. I behaved dishonourably. I went off the rails for the very first time in my life and it has been a sobering experience. I deeply regret everything which has happened between us.'

Georgie's appetite had vanished. She surveyed the exquisitely arranged meal through swimming eyes. She was suffering from this truly appalling urge to leap out of bed and put her arms round him. Lord, but she had it bad! Here he was practically on his knees and she didn't even have the gumption to feel any sense of vindicated satisfaction. He had insulted her, threatened her, deprived her of her freedom, and now he was saying sorry in the only way he could. And since humility came about as naturally to Rafael as walking on water would come to her, she knew exactly what this approach had to be costing him in terms of pride.

'Fine. Apology accepted,' she said with forced lightness.

'That is very generous of you.'

It suddenly occurred to her that, in giving way to her shell-shocked emotions earlier, she had been childishly self-indulgent. They had made love, a development she now saw as inevitable. And Rafael had not swept her off to bed without her enthusiastic encouragement. She forced her head up, dealing him a glance from beneath thick copper lashes, and shrugged a narrow shoulder. 'Least said, soonest mended,' she dismissed, quoting her late grandmother.

Lustrous dark eyes rested on her with incisive intensity. 'You are taking this very well!'

I'll be out of here tomorrow.

'Why not?' Georgie contrived another shrug, even managed a faint smile, and felt immensely proud of herself until she realised that she was finding it incredibly hard to drag her gaze from his darkly handsome features. Memory roamed relentlessly back a few hours and a surge of heat dampened her skin, interfered with her breathing and sent her heartbeat into shameless acceleration. In bed, he was her every fantasy fulfilled, and the instant that thought came to her she drowned in self-loathing.

'*Bueno*.' Rafael expelled his breath in a hiss. Tension sizzled from his stance in palpable waves. From the foot of the bed he watched her, his magnificent physique visibly taut. His hard jawline clenched, a tiny pulse tugging at the corner of his unsmiling mouth.

The silence smouldered. Georgie fingered a prawn off her starter and munched defiantly at it, her cheeks still hot as hellfire from her last thought.

'Then allow me the very great honour of asking you to become my wife,' Rafael breathed, with an abruptness that brutally shattered the tense silence.

CHAPTER SEVEN

HALFWAY to success in pursuit of a second luscious prawn, Georgie stilled and looked up, met shimmering golden eyes fiercely pinned to her. She tried and failed to swallow. Her wide violet gaze clung to him in rampant disbelief.

'I'm an angel now,' she whispered in shock.

'*Que*?' Rafael stared darkly back at her.

'You're not serious?' Georgie framed weakly.

'I have already spoken to Father Tomás.'

Georgie blinked rapidly at the calm announcement. 'You've *what*?'

'Or if you would prefer I could contact an English minister I am acquainted with in La Paz.'

Numbly, Georgie shook her head. Rafael gazed steadily back at her, impervious, it seemed, to her disbelief. She drew in a slow, shaky breath, her heart thumping noisily in her eardrums. 'I just don't believe I'm hearing this... You don't want to marry me!'

'Had I had more faith in you four years ago, we would already have been man and wife,' Rafael drawled in a tone of finality.

'But that's got nothing to do with *now*.'

'Georgie... I want to marry you.'

Georgie dragged unwillingly fascinated eyes from his forceful gaze and sighed heavily. 'When you said we were from different cultures, you weren't joking. I suppose you think you *have* to marry me because—well—because we slept together.'

'I want the right to share that bed with you every night,' Rafael murmured softly.

Her skin warmed. She didn't question the overwhelmingly strong attraction between them but she sincerely doubted that in any other circumstances it would have prompted Rafael to offer marriage after making love to her. He was feeling guilty. Rafael, who prided himself on his principles, his sense of honour and his excellent judgement, had just weathered the discovery that he was human after all. Not perfect, not without flaw...and both his manner and his appearance told her just how savaging that revelation had been.

So here he was now, offering the only reparation he could. Marriage. He would marry her because he had slept with her. He would marry her because he had been her first lover. And perhaps he would also marry her because he had already told her that that had been his intent four years ago. Not for any other reasons. Not because any romanticised view of her lingered from the past. No such illusions could remain after what Rafael had believed about her for so long. But, regardless of all that, Rafael would force himself to make the ultimate sacrifice. He believed that he *owed* her that wedding-ring. For a split-second she felt so corrosively bitter that it physically hurt to breathe.

'We're just not suited,' Georgie muttered. 'But I do appreciate the thought.' It was a lie. Suddenly she hated him for his precious code of honour and decency, light-years away from the values of the more liberated society in which she had been raised. Such a proposal was no compliment. 'Thanks, but no thanks.'

'It wasn't just a thought,' Rafael rebutted tautly.

'No, I expect it took a lot of macho courage for you to ask a woman you don't like and don't respect to become your wife,' Georgie responded, equally tautly.

'But the point is, I don't want to marry you anyway, so it wasn't necessary.'

'That is not how I regard you now.' His retort was level. 'I made a very grave error of judgement four years ago——'

A knife-edged laugh was torn from Georgie. 'An error of judgement!' she repeated helplessly, and looked heavenward, unable to escape the recollection of how badly she had been hurt by the fall-out.

A dark rise of blood had accentuated his high cheekbones, but he held her evasive gaze unflinchingly. 'Think of it from my point of view——'

'*Your* point of view?' she gasped incredulously.

'I knew that Steve did not look on you as a sister. I was aware that he was sexually attracted to you——'

Georgie threw her head back, her disgust unhidden. 'Are you still trying to twist the facts? That night, when Steve suddenly grabbed me and kissed me, he had had too much to drink. He was upset because he had had a row with his girlfriend. It was just one of those stupid, crazy things that people do sometimes on impulse and it meant nothing!'

Rafael dealt her a slashing glance. 'You only see what you want to see, Georgie...'

'And what's that supposed to mean?'

His expressive mouth flattened into a compressed white line. 'Steve,' he breathed tautly. 'You still love him as a brother, as a member of your family?'

Georgie frowned, unable to understand his need to state the obvious. 'Naturally, we're close. Why wouldn't we be?' she demanded.

Rafael was very still, his dark features oddly tense and austere as he studied her. There was a long pause. Then he shrugged a shoulder with a grim air of finality. 'When I saw you in his arms, how do you think I felt?'

Georgie compressed her lips. She was a little surprised by his continuing hostility towards her stepbrother in spite of the fact that he now knew the truth. Didn't he now appreciate that he had misjudged Steve just as badly as he had misjudged her? Then, no doubt, Rafael still blamed Steve for that stupid kiss he had witnessed. 'I expect you were as taken aback seeing it as I was when it happened,' she conceded grudgingly.

'I was in love with you!' Rafael bit out with raw emphasis, and her head jerked up, her eyes widening. '"Taken aback" does not begin to describe my feelings that night or the following day!'

'I find it very hard to believe that you loved me,' she admitted.

'Don't be more stupid than you can help!' Rafael slung her a glittering golden glance of exasperation. 'For what other reason would I have wanted to marry you?'

She swallowed hard. The idea that he had loved her four years ago merely piled on the agony. If he had loved her, he hadn't trusted her, and he had walked away without a backward glance. 'Well, it doesn't really matter now, does it?'

'So you keep telling me.'

'We've got nothing more to say to each other.'

'Another platitude,' Rafael derided, a gathering storm of anger lightening his gaze to gold. 'And what platitude will you employ if you find that you are carrying my child in a few weeks? Are we all to be treated to the "Oops, gosh, I didn't think" response that you seem to believe covers every eventuality?'

Georgie stared back at him, pale as death.

Rafael absorbed her stunned response with grim eyes. 'No, I didn't protect you. An inexcusable omission, but in all that excitement the risk only crossed my mind for one second, and I foolishly assumed that you would still be on the contraceptive pill. The look on your face tells me you are not... and why should you have been?' he demanded with a sardonic edge. 'You had no reason to take such a precaution.'

Georgie licked at her dry lips in a flickering motion, briefly lost in a stricken vision of single parenthood, unemployment and family horror. Then her fevered imagination steadied as she performed some frantic calculations as to the date of her last period, but there was no great comfort to be found there. Whether she liked it or not, there was a slight risk of pregnancy. Not a large risk, she hurriedly consoled herself—at least, she didn't think so.

'It's not very likely,' she asserted breathlessly.

'But not impossible?'

'Nothing's impossible, but I would say the chances are probably slim to none.'

'The eternal optimist.' Rafael slung her a scathing smile and then he asked her bluntly when exactly she could expect to know whether or not she was pregnant.

'That's none of your——'

'If you're pregnant, it will be very much my business,' he cut in drily.

Tight-mouthed, she obliged the information.

'I would say computing a risk factor of slim to none is suicidally optimistic,' he returned drily. 'And I have no intention of waiting to find out!'

Exhausted by all the stress, Georgie sighed. Suddenly she understood another motivation behind his stated desire to marry her. The mere threat of a Berganza being born on the metaphorical wrong side of the blanket was a shattering one for a male of Rafael's breeding. And it was typical of him to look only on the darkest side of the equation. Where Georgie instinctively expected not to be further punished for her recklessness by an unplanned pregnancy, Rafael probably expected triplets.

'God couldn't be so cruel,' she mumbled helplessly.

'Every child is a gift from God,' Rafael asserted with ferocious bite. 'That is why we will get married as soon as possible.'

A hysterical giggle lodged like a giant stone in Georgie's throat. 'I went to bed with you. I didn't sign my whole life away!'

'It was my fault. I seduced you.'

Georgie's sensitive stomach heaved and she looked at him with incredulous eyes. 'Women of my age don't get seduced—revolting word,' she grimaced. 'I take responsibility for my own actions.'

'But you're dangerously impulsive. You always were.'

Incensed by the unwelcome seed of reality to that assessment, Georgie stiffened defensively. 'Fortunately, I'm not impulsive enough to agree to a marriage which neither one of us wants! I'm not wrecking my life over one stupid mistake!'

'It is a mistake which you will have to learn to live with,' Rafael told her, striding towards the door, his hard-edged profile unyielding.

'In a pig's eye, I will!' Georgie launched back at him. 'And don't think you can bully me into changing my mind.'

The door flipped shut. She slumped back on the pillows. He had proposed to her, which was rather a joke. After all, he had already embarked on arrangements for a wedding! Typical Rafael. He always ran a one-horse race. And presumably he had expected her to rush breathlessly into agreement. But he knew she had loved him four years ago, was undoubtedly aware that she would have married him like a shot had he asked her then.

Like any girl, she had dreamt about marrying the man she loved. But that was then . . . and this was now, when she was a whole lot older and wiser. Rafael was not in love with her. She found it so hard to believe that he had *ever* loved her, so icily controlled had he been at their final meeting. Wouldn't a man in love have raged and stormed at her in bitter fury and jealousy? Or were such base but supremely human emotions beneath Rafael and the self-discipline he prided himself on?

She remembered that last meeting in his apartment so well.

Rafael had been ice while she did all the humiliating things he had reminded her of just yesterday. She *had* wept and begged. She *had* pleaded with him to listen to her. She *had* begged him not to leave her. Why had she gone to such lengths without the smallest encouragement to do so?

She had been passionately in love with him, and what Rafael had believed he had interrupted at Danny's apartment had been so ludicrous. Then, of course, she had not been aware that Rafael had also seen Steve kissing her. And naturally she would not have referred to that embarrassing slip of Steve's. She had calmed down by then, was very fond of her stepbrother and, if family loyalty hadn't kept her quiet, discomfiture over that embrace certainly would have done. Looking back, it merely seemed a silly storm in a teacup. It would never have occurred to her that Rafael could have seen them.

When she woke up the next morning, she pulled on jeans and a tailored white shirt with roll-back cuffs. No more games. There was no longer any need for games in the cause of self-defence. There was a need for calm and common sense. Presumably Rafael, a decent interval after all that positively gothic talk about honour and principles, would now be calmer and more reasonable too.

But, as she descended the stairs, her carefully prepared cool was instantly smashed by Rafael's appearance in the hall. He was dressed for riding in skin-tight beige breeches and a black polo shirt. Every superbly fit line of his gorgeous body was smoothly delineated, his lazy stride laced with an utterly unselfconscious animal sensuality. Quite simply, his sheer physical impact stopped her in her tracks. Lean, mean and magnificent. Her mouth ran dry.

'*Buenos días, querida.*' Bracing a polished leather boot on the bottom step, Rafael treated her to a raking, overwhelmingly male appraisal which made her skin heat. 'Do you still ride?'

'Only a handful of times since I went to college. I couldn't afford it.'

'It isn't a skill you forget. I'll take you out with me tomorrow.' Somehow he contrived to make the invitation sound as intimate as a siesta in a double bed.

Georgie tensed. 'I won't be here tomorrow.'

'You think not?' Reaching out, he tugged her forward in one smooth motion and encircled her in his arms. Still standing a step higher, Georgie found herself facing him levelly.

'Rafael . . . no!' she gasped feverishly.

He penetrated her anxiously parted lips with his tongue and she shuddered, electrified by the intense eroticism of his opening assault.

'Closer,' he urged, his breath fanning her cheek, smouldering golden eyes burning down into hers as his hands cupped the swell of her buttocks and lifted her into intimate connection with the hard thrust of his arousal. '*Sí* . . . like *that* . . .'

He crushed her mouth under his and she was electrified by the hunger which leapt into response inside her. Keen and fierce as a knife, that voracious hunger cleaved through her flesh. Her breasts swelled and ached and her nipples pinched into painfully sensitive points. She arched her back like a sensuous cat, desperate for more sensation, her head thrown back, her hands wound round his neck.

'If you had been in my bed when I woke up, I wouldn't be suffering this way. I would be satisfied,' Rafael murmured huskily, rubbing an abrasive cheek intimately against the tender skin of her throat and then reaching up teasingly to tug at her ear-lobe with sharp teeth, and if he hadn't been holding her up at that point she honestly believed she would have folded into quivering female surrender at his feet. By that stage, her entire body was on fire.

'Ah . . . we have company.' Swinging her down off the step and turning, Rafael lowered her to the floor, but kept his arms linked round her, her spine welded to the warm, hard wall of his chest.

'Company?' Georgie echoed dazedly.

'Allow me to introduce you to my father's eldest sister, Tía Paola. I know she will want you to address her as one of the family.'

Georgie's gaze fell on a beaming, plump little woman with white hair and twinkling dark eyes. In spite of her shock that Rafael should be entertaining unexpected visitors, and relatives at that, she found herself smiling back. Tía Paola had that kind of face. She moved forward to clasp Georgie's hands warmly and murmur a greeting.

'And, of course, Tía's ward—Beatriz Herrera León.' Georgie's attention was drawn by the young woman coming down the stairs towards them, a tall designer-clad brunette of quite stunning looks and presence. Liquid dark eyes regarded her with faint amusement as the introduction was performed. And, all of a sudden, Georgie felt horribly aware of her casual clothing, swollen mouth and thoroughly mussed hair.

'I am very pleased to meet you, Señorita Morrison,' Beatriz said with cool formality.

'Miss León,' Georgie murmured.

'Your *novia* is very beautiful, Rafael.' The brunette's gracious smile embraced both of them but her eyes remained cold as charity.

'*Novia*?' Georgie parroted, that being one of the very few Spanish words she was familiar with, thanks to María Cristina. It meant bride or fiancée.

Rafael's arms tightened around her. 'Excuse me, we have some calls to make before breakfast.'

Georgie was dragged—there was no other word for it—into Rafael's library. He closed the door and swung round to survey her with hooded dark eyes.

'*Novia*?' Georgie said again, an entire octave higher.

'Tía Paola has arrived to act as your chaperon.'

Hands on hips, Georgie stared back at him, aghast. 'My *what*?'

'Whatever happens now, I naturally wish to safeguard your reputation. My family is very traditional,' Rafael drawled without apology. 'In bringing you here alone, I compromised you. Tía's presence will silence any adverse comment.'

Georgie pushed an unsteady hand through her mass of vibrant hair. 'They think I'm going to marry you, don't they?'

'You will,' Rafael responded with complete conviction.

'I told you last night that I wouldn't even consider it!' Georgie stalked across the room in turmoil, raw tension edging every bitten-out word. She spun back to him. 'And I'm not likely to change my mind. All you're going to do is embarrass yourself with your family.'

'Not at all. If no wedding takes place, they will sigh and say I've wriggled off the hook yet again——'

'Make a habit of that, do you?' Georgie couldn't resist stabbing.

'I have never raised expectations I had no intention of fulfilling.'

Once you raised mine. But she didn't say it. The biting pain still lingered, and with it a tortured vulnerability. She felt torn in two. One half of her, what she deemed to be the intelligent half, desperately wanted to go home to sanity, but the other half of her was savaged by the sure knowledge that she would never see Rafael again.

'I won't marry you,' she said stonily.

'I want you more than any woman alive,' Rafael intoned with a wine-dark harshness underlying his accented drawl. 'Your beauty glows like a vibrant flame in this dim room. You look at me with those passionately expressive violet eyes and that enticing sultry mouth and I burn for you. If such hunger isn't a basis for marriage, what is?'

A quiver ran through her slender length. The hair at the nape of her neck prickled. The very sound of his voice could make her ache. In the smouldering silence, the tension was suffocating. Sex, she thought in shame, as her breasts stirred in response beneath her cotton bra. Every skin-cell in her treacherous body was poised on the peak of anticipation.

'It's not enough for me,' she said jerkily, lifting her chin, forcing back a response she despised.

Blazing golden eyes clashed with hers, and for an instant she couldn't move, couldn't breathe, couldn't even think straight. He was lounging on the corner of his desk, as terrifyingly beautiful as a hungry tiger, ready to spring. Her heart clenched. The fierce primal power of him sprang out at her in an aggressive wave. Last night's humility hadn't survived to greet the dawn. The driving force of his strong will was stamped in every hard bronzed feature.

'I could make it enough,' he asserted.

But I would be the lover, not the loved. Her pride could not tolerate that mortifying image. A flush ran up beneath her magnolia-perfect skin. She would be the toy in his bed, just another possession to a male already bountifully blessed with life's richest possessions. She saw how his natural arrogance had altered the reasoning she had believed she understood mere hours earlier. Forget the reparation angle! Rafael was now telling her that he was freely choosing to marry her for the sexual pleasure he expected her to give him.

Maybe that had been what he called love four years ago. Desire. A desire honed to a fine lustful edge by her youthful unavailability when they had first met. Hadn't he admitted that himself? That he had never had to wait for anything he wanted before? And she hadn't distinguished herself by making him wait this time, had she? No, she had been an easy conquest, betrayed by passion and need and love. And, if she married Rafael, she would betray herself over and over again in his bed until self-loathing spread through her like a cancer.

Almost clumsily she folded her arms, as if to hold in the fiery emotions surging up inside her. 'No,' she said again, her voice taut with unbearable strain.

'And will you be able to live with that choice?' Rafael asked in a velvet-soft purr of enquiry. 'For I will certainly marry someone in the near future. I am of an age to want a wife and a family.'

Georgie turned deathly white. That one casually cruel statement was like a knife thudding into her unprotected breast.

Rafael held her darkened violet eyes with savage amusement twisting in his hard mouth. 'Sometimes, I am a primitive bastard, *es verdad*? But you're taxing my patience. Every jealous, possessive bone in that exquisite body of yours revolts at the mere idea of me marrying another woman——'

'*No!*' she gasped strickenly, shattered by his instinctive cruelty and the cool insight which had made him use that particular weapon against her.

Rafael lifted his handsome dark head and angled a sizzling smile over her. 'Had we more time at our disposal, I would have been more diplomatic, more sensitive——'

'You arrogant swine!' she shot from between gritted teeth.

'I will not allow your need to punish me to come between us.' Eyes black as night surveyed her impenetrably from below lush ebony lashes. 'Nor will I crawl. Remember this, *querida* you were not the only one to suffer four years ago, you were not the only one whose pride and emotions were injured...'

Georgie stiffened, deeply disturbed by the assertion. Honesty forced her to admit that she had been less than generous in her ability to see those events from his side of the fence. But then, deep down inside, she still believed that if Rafael had really cared about her he would have betrayed his emotions more and he would at least have *tried* to listen to her. Was that so unreasonable? And what did it matter now, anyway? she asked herself with helpless bitterness. Even if he had loved her then, to the best of his seemingly limited ability, he wasn't in love with her now. If it wasn't for the sizzling animal sexuality he emitted as naturally as some men simply breathed, Rafael wouldn't be half so keen to marry her.

'Breakfast,' he sighed with sudden impatience.

Only as he straightened and moved forward did Georgie see what reposed on his desk. She darted forward, an exclamation on her lips. 'My bag!'

'*Sí* ... I had informed the hotel manager of your loss. The driver returned the bag to your hotel and it was conveyed here late last night with my guests. Check the contents.'

Georgie was already in the midst of doing so. Her passport was there ... and so was her money. She went weak with relief.

'Most people prefer the—er—convenience of travellers' cheques,' Rafael remarked.

'I just didn't have time to get them before the flight out...OK?' Georgie demanded with belligerence. 'I want to give that cab-driver a reward——'

'It's already taken care of.'

'I'm sorry I called him a thief,' Georgie muttered.

'He may well have been tempted, but the fear that you would describe him, and might even have the registration of his cab, may have influenced him. Who knows?' Rafael returned with rich cynicism.

Georgie drew in a deep, sustaining breath and lifted her head. 'There's no problem now. I can go home...'

'But before you leave I will naturally demand the certainty that you are not carrying my child,' Rafael decreed, his beautifully shaped mouth compressing into a forbidding line. 'And you cannot give me that assurance yet.'

Frustrated fury hurtled through her. 'Last night, you admitted that you regretted everything you had done!'

'That does not mean I now give you the freedom to behave with the foresight of a five-year-old,' Rafael delivered with sardonic bite.

Rage roared through Georgie in a blinding, seething surge. Her hands clenched into fists by her sides. 'Don't you dare put me down like that! I didn't ask to come here! I wanted nothing to do with you!'

'Then why when you woke up in that cell did you look at me with such hunger?' Rafael sliced back with indolent cool.

'I did not look at you like that!' Georgie seethed in outrage.

'And maybe you don't recall smirking and flexing those truly fabulous legs like offensive weapons on the drive back to La Paz either?'

'I do not *smirk*...and if you can't keep your lousy libido under control, that is not my problem!' she practically spat back.

'You got exactly the effect you wanted. I was ignoring you and you didn't like it.'

'How dare you say that?'

'Four years ago, you were exactly the same. A natural-born tease——'

'You bastard!' Georgie was so outraged that she could hardly get the words out.

'If I ended up with the wrong impression, ask yourself how much the act you put on for my benefit contributed,' Rafael retorted drily. 'If any teenage daughter of mine tried to walk out of the door on a date in a plunge neckline with a pelmet-length skirt, suspenders and an ankle chain, I'd paddle her backside!'

'I was trying to look sophisticated, you insensitive toad!' Her voice quivered with a mortification which merely increased her fury. 'I suppose you'd have found me more exciting if I'd been covered from throat to toe like a nun!'

'You would certainly have been more presentable in public. And less confusing in private,' Rafael completed in a strained undertone, his starkly handsome features taut with an amalgam of emotions she was too angry to read.

Georgie had worked herself up to such a pitch of ungovernable fury that she was beyond speech. Snatching at her bag, throwing him a splintering purple glare of sheer loathing, she headed for the door.

'Georgie...' Rafael murmured very softly to her rigid back, 'if you treat my aunt to a temperamental display, you will discover that my temper is far more dangerous than your own.'

Her teeth actually ground together. The note of cool warning in that assurance nearly sent her into orbit.

Without turning her head, she walked out of the room, across the hall and out of the house. Another minute, another single minute in contact with that hateful tongue of his and she would have been up for murder! Aflame with rage, she stalked across the beautiful gardens like a tigress on the prowl.

He had no right to keep her here against her wishes! With flaring eyes, she shot a glance at the bare helicopter landing-pad and stalked on. There had to be some other way off the *estancia*. Family and guests arrived by air. What about everybody else? On horseback...on foot...or on four wheels? Her attention fell on the four-wheel-drive parked over beside a couple of other toughly designed vehicles. Well, well, well, she thought, glancing around the vast deserted asphalt expanse surrounding her.

Obviously there was somewhere to go out there on four wheels. Strolling over, Georgie glanced in and saw the keys in the ignition. It took her one split-second to make her decision. Her only other hope of escape was making a scene in the presence of Rafael's aunt, and she was very reluctant to subject that sweet little old lady to the shocking revelation that her nephew was virtually imprisoning his supposed *novia* on the *estancia*.

Sliding into the driver's seat, Georgie wasted no more time. Rafael could send her clothes on after her, and if he didn't bother, escape would still be coming cheap at the price. She had her money and her passport and that was all she required. The engine fired and she checked the petrol-gauge. The tank was full and there was a bottle full of water lying on the floor in front of the passenger seat. She drove off down the asphalt lane with an almost crazed sense of release exploding inside her, her palms damply gripping the leather steering-wheel.

The lane came to an end only a mile out, but the lie of the ground in all directions as far as the purple snow-capped Cordillera mountains in the distance was flat and would provide no problems for a four-wheel-drive. Even so, the lush grass of the savannah provided a less smooth surface than she had expected and, where it was broken up by scrubland, the going was even rougher, but Georgie was nothing if not persistent.

The heat was intense, even with the air-conditioning running full blast. Perspiration ran down between her breasts and her lower body felt stifled in the jeans she was wearing. The very occasional tree was all that interrupted the monotony of the landscape. A sense of her own isolation began to creep over her. She stopped to moisten her dry mouth and only when she had tilted the bottle back did she discover that what she had gaily assumed to be water was, in fact, some form of tonsil-searing alcohol. Choking, tears springing to her eyes, she threw the bottle aside in disgust.

So far, her assumption that there had to be some form of settlement within a couple of hours' drive of the estancia had yet to be fulfilled. She kept a careful eye on the petrol-gauge. If she didn't hit somewhere soon, she would be forced to turn back and the realisation galled her, flattening her foot down more heavily on the accelerator. Then, far to her left, she saw a clump of trees and something pink shimmering . . . a rooftop?

Damn, damn, damn, she thought a little while later, watching the graceful flock of pink flamingos round the lagoon take flight in a gorgeous spray of heady colour against the deep blue sky. It was the most beautiful sight and, even in the mood Georgie was in, she responded to that beauty. Killing the engine, because she was in severe need of a break, she slid out into the enveloping heat, flexing her stiff muscles and tugging her shirt out of her jeans in a vain attempt to cool off.

She was going to have to turn back. Rage had been dissipated by exertion. Another one up to you, Rafael, she reflected in raw frustration, strolling towards the shore of the lagoon. The water shimmered like a spun-glass enticement. She was so hot... Then something shifted in the corner of her eye.

'Oh, my lord...' Georgie watched what she had dimly taken for a floating log metamorphose into a big, ugly alligator heading her way. Her stomach heaved with a kind of sick, terrified fascination and then instinct shifted her frozen limbs and she ran like a maniac back to the car.

'You can keep the local wildlife, Rafael,' she mumbled, winding up the window as the creature was joined by another, their horrible little stumpy legs beginning to plough through the grass.

Without any further ado, she turned the car and started back. She had been driving about an hour when the engine began to make unhealthy spluttering sounds. Within a mile the vehicle coughed to a final halt, and none of her efforts could get it going again. The heat built around her and she was forced to take another swig of the noxious brew in the bottle. Liquid was liquid, she reasoned.

The emptiness of the savannah was surreal. It would have been terrifying had Georgie not had such immense faith in Rafael, who would find her if only out of a need to strangle her with his bare hands. She rested her head back, breathing shallowly, and waited miserably to be rescued. Another hour went by on leaden feet. Her optimism took a sudden dip on the recollection that the helicopter hadn't been at the *estancia* and finding her without aerial reconnaissance might be like looking for a needle in a haystack.

Better wed than dead, she thought, staggering out of the inferno-like heat of the car interior when she could bear it no longer. Severe sunburn as opposed to suffo-cation—not a lot of choice there. It was his fault. He had driven her to this. He had made her desperate. And yet what real effort had she made to escape before now?

Had she lifted the phone beside her bed to call Steve, who was almost certainly home again by now? Had she contacted the British Embassy? Had she tried to bribe his helicopter pilot? Had she thrown herself on Father Garcia's mercy? No, she had rolled back to Rafael like a homing pigeon...and gone to bed with him. At no stage, she realised numbly, had she made a single realistic attempt to free herself. Until now, and then it had taken naked rage to push her to the attempt.

In the shadow of the car, she sank down on the scrubby grass. When she first saw the speck on the shimmering horizon, she thought it was a bird, undoubtedly of the vulture variety, scenting a banquet. Then she realised it was a horse and rider. On a slope, they briefly stilled, silhouetted against the skyline. It was Rafael. She *knew* it, *felt* it in her bones.

Nobody else but Rafael could possibly look that good on a horse. A big black Arabian, which ploughed across the rolling plain with power, stamina and extraordinary natural beauty. Her heart rushed up into her torturously dry mouth. And I said no, she thought, deliriously impressionable as sheer relief washed over her.

CHAPTER EIGHT

GEORGIE rose shakily upright. The stallion thundered to a halt, reined back with powerful ease twenty feet from her. Incandescent golden eyes smouldered over her hot, crumpled length, patently checking out her physical condition. Rafael dug out a two-way radio and spoke into it in fast Spanish, but his compelling gaze didn't roam from her for a second. It was curiously like being handcuffed and tied up.

Immobile, Georgie looked back at him in the simmering silence that was laden with menace. He was mad, of course he was mad. So he would say 'I told you so' in a variety of cutting, utterly unpleasant ways, because nobody said that phrase with greater satisfaction than Rafael. Rafael loved to be proved right. And, like it or not, she would take it all on the chin for once.

Setting off on a whim into an unknown, hostile terrain as featureless as this one had been the behaviour of a total idiot and no doubt she deserved everything she had coming to her. But the main reason Georgie would let him shout at her was the intense and naked relief she had seen etched in those gorgeous eyes as he visibly reassured himself that she was unharmed.

Rafael had been worried sick about her safety, probably far more worried than she had been on her own behalf. That dark, brooding temperament of his did not have a shred of her own invariably sunny, optimistic outlook. Rafael always expected the worst. A fat alligator snoozing beside a heap of picked-bare bones wouldn't have surprised him. That certainty sent a pained tenderness washing through her.

He dismounted in one fluid movement and tossed a water bottle to her without even needing to be asked. It landed on the grass at her feet. Lifting it with an unsteady hand, Georgie swiftly took advantge of the ice-cold precious water within. Then, beginning to feel positively intimidated by the continuing unnatural silence, she moistened her throat and her brow with the cool liquid.

'*Madre de Dios...*' Rafael growled in a seething tone of savagery she had never heard from him before. 'You are the most stupid bitch it has ever been my misfortune to meet!'

Gulping, Georgie nodded and wondered if it was too soon to test out a grateful smile.

'What do you have to say for yourself?' He strode forward, a dark flush delineating his sculpted cheekbones.

'My hero...?' Her voice emerged all squeaky and strange.

And that was it. Rafael went rigid, and then his narrowed eyes bit into her like grappling hooks and he reached for her with one savage hand, roughly grasping the front of her shirt to propel her closer. 'You think this is funny?' he splintered down at her from his vastly superior height, in a surge of such undisciplined rage that his diction was destroyed. 'Every man available has been engaged on an all-out search for you! And what do you dare to say to me when I find you?'

'Sorry...I am very sorry, but it's not my fault the blasted car broke down, is it?'

'It was in for repair.'

'Oh... Well, I didn't know that,' Georgie muttered weakly.

'Where were you going?' he demanded with raw aggression.

'I thought there'd be a village, another ranch... I didn't mean to cause anyone any inconvenience... I mean...' Sentenced to stillness, her stomach turning over, Georgie watched for some encouraging sign that his rage was levelling out, and failed to receive it.

'Oops...gosh...I didn't think.' His smouldering eyes flashed fierily over her drawn face as she visibly winced at the slashing derision he revealed. 'There is nothing for hundreds of miles——'

'*Hundreds* of miles?' With difficulty, Georgie swallowed.

'No drinkable water, no source of food, poisonous snakes——'

'I got chased by an alligator,' she told him, hoping that confirmation of his expectations would cool him down.

'An alligator... You got as far as the lagoon?' Rafael roared at her a full octave higher. 'You stopped, obviously you got out of the car... for what?'

'I was hot and——'

'You were going to swim with piranhas and electric eels?'

'It never crossed my mind for a moment!' Georgie swore vehemently, shuddering with horror.

He spat something at her in Spanish and shook her again. Two buttons flew off her shirt. 'You did,' Rafael condemned, in so much rage that he could scarcely vocalise the contradiction. 'You did think of swimming! It's written all over you! In the name of God, do you have an IQ in single figures? You need a baby-sitter and a playpen, not a husband!'

Trying with a trembling hand to hold the edges of her shirt together, Georgie went rigid under the onslaught of his abuse. Taking it on the chin as a policy of non-aggressive negotiation vanished.

'Now, you listen here——' she began hotly.

'Shut up!' Rafael seethed down at her, his golden features a mask of fury. 'You took off in a tantrum and I, Rafael Rodriguez Berganza, do not listen to a woman who behaves like a spoilt, reckless child!'

'Get stuffed, you superior SOB!' Georgie hissed.

'What did you call me?'

'Gone deaf suddenly? Lost that wonderful English?' Georgie threw back wrathfully.

Trembling, he stared down at her, the explosive tension in every line of his powerful body hitting her in waves of palpable heat. Burning eyes dug into her. 'If I had married you four years ago, you would have respect for me——'

'No doubt you would have beaten it in with a whip... just your style!' Georgie screeched back.

'I have no need of a whip with you.' His seething gaze dropped to the heaving curves of her full breasts, visible between the parted edges of her shirt. And then he dealt her a dark explicit glance that sent her heartbeat racing up the scale.

Georgie was not slow on the uptake. Instant awareness linked with disbelief assailed her. 'No...' she said thickly.

He coiled a booted foot round the back of her legs and tipped her down on the grass with such fluid ease and speed that she didn't have a hope of evading the manoeuvre. A second later, he came down on top of her, one hand reaching instantly for the snap of her jeans. 'We'll save the Ferrari for some other time... but here, now, on Berganza soil... this is for *me*!'

Georgie was so shocked that he had her halfway out of her jeans before she made even a partial recovery. 'Have you gone mad?' she shrieked.

Her jeans were cast aside. He knelt astride her and slid down the zip on his riding breeches. Georgie stared up at him with a dropped jaw. He shed his polo shirt, flexing powerful muscles that rippled smoothly across his hair-roughened chest. She shivered in the heat, her nostrils flaring at the musky male scent of him.

'Rafael...?'

'You are mine...like the land.'

The absolute possession in the statement was primitive in its intensity. Shimmering golden eyes flamed over her with devouring desire, and heat flooded her every skin-cell in a wanton burst of instant response. He might as well have lit a torch inside her. Her teeth gritted as what remained of sanity sought to be heard. 'No!' she protested as he lowered his arrogant dark head.

'You are my woman.' Lean but frighteningly strong hands cupped her cheekbones. His burnished gaze held hers fiercely. 'And by the time I have finished with you, you will know it too,' he swore with unapologetic savagery.

'I don't like it when you get macho,' Georgie said in breathless defiance.

'Liar...I excite the hell out of you,' Rafael derided. 'I'm still waiting to qualify for a knee in the groin!'

He very nearly did, but with a raw burst of laughter he evaded her furious attempt to make good that oversight. He stilled her with all the power of his superior strength. And then he took her mouth with a ravishing passion that stole her soul. She was stunned into submission by the white-hot hunger he unleashed on her. One hand fiercely knotted in her hair, he plundered her readily parted lips, every stab of his exploring tongue teaching her the depth of his need.

With his other hand, he wrenched her bra out of his impatient path, curving hard fingers over the exposed mounds of her staining breasts. With an earthy groan, he touched and tantalised the distended pink nipples which betrayed the extent of her response to him. The raw intensity of what he was making her feel excited her beyond bearing. Her fingers drove into his raven hair in ecstasy as he suckled strongly at her sensitive breasts. Her whole body was a melting river of liquid flame.

As his head lifted from her breasts, she drew him back to her, wild for the hot, hard possession of his mouth again. Her darkened eyes clung to his and her arms closed convulsively round him, adoring hands splaying across the long golden sweep of his satin-smooth back, and she knew it then—knew that whether it was madness or not he was everything to her, everything she had ever wanted, everything she had ever needed, everything she had ever craved in her most secret thoughts.

With a tormentingly light touch, he explored the moist silken heat of her, and tiny sounds she couldn't hold back began to escape her. Her fingers dug into his powerful shoulders, her entire body racked by an intolerable pleasure that only made her cry out for more. He pulled free of her and parted her thighs and she shivered violently, desperate for the ache he had aroused to be satisfied by the hard thrust of his masculinity.

Abruptly she tensed in shock as his silky hair brushed her taut stomach and she felt his mouth caress her in the most intimate way of all.

'No!' she gasped, her eyes flying wide.

His hands tightened inexorably on her slender thighs, preventing her withdrawal. '*Sí*...I want you out of your mind with pleasure,' he murmured softly.

The experience fulfilled his every intention. One moment she was rigid with tension, the next lost in a world of physical sensation so intense that she was overwhelmed. She writhed and moaned, helpless in the grip of her own body's unbridled response. She gasped his name pleadingly at a peak of quivering urgency.

'*Ahora . . .* now.'

He lifted himself and plunged inside her in one dev-astating thrust of possession. Her every sense was screaming for the release that only he could give. Her nails dug into his back and then he was moving on her, inside her, with every powerful stroke of his hips re-inforcing his dominance. As the heat of passion spiralled out of control, she cried out in ecstasy as he drove her to a shattering climax.

Still in a satiated daze, Georgie lifted her heavy eyelids. He reminded her of a primitive golden god, surveying a pagan sacrifice spread out before him. An aching vul-nerability swept her as she collided with tawny tiger eyes that revealed nothing of his thoughts.

'Rafael?' Involuntarily her hand reached up to smooth one hard cheekbone.

'*Enamorada...*' With a curiously harsh laugh, he took her startled, reddened mouth with his own and it began all over again...

What have I done? What have I done? The anguished question rang in ceaseless refrain inside her head as she fumbled her way back into her clothes with hands that just weren't responding with their usual efficiency. She felt shattered, drained, desperately confused, all at one and the same time. Her mind touched on the raw passion Rafael had employed to attain her submission, and something shrivelled up and died inside her.

He strolled across the flattened grass and gently re-moved her hands from the crumpled shirt she was at-tempting to tie closed. He peeled the sleeves back down her arms in silence and strode back to his horse. From a saddlebag, he produced a polo shirt, similar to the one he wore himself. Her cheeks burning, she caught it as he tossed it to her, and hurriedly dived into its voluminous folds.

He vaulted back into the saddle and reached down to pull her up in front of him. She was so tense that he had to flatten a hand to her abdomen to force her into relaxed contact with his hard body. She trembled, stricken by the sheer force of her physical awareness of him now.

'Is that why you want to marry me?' She couldn't hold the question back any longer, though the instant she voiced it she wished she had kept her mouth shut.

'*No entiendo, querida,*' he drawled.

He understood. He understood damned fine, but he would make her spell it out.

'The sex—is it worth a wedding-ring?' Georgie demanded, grateful he couldn't see the stinging tears lashing her eyes.

'You can be very crude...' he murmured lazily against her ear.

'Put it down to my lack of experience.'

'Sexually we are a match made in heaven—am I to deny that?'

If the past hours of fevered passion had taught her anything, they had taught her that she could not deny him. But she wanted more, she wanted so much more than the confirmation of the raw hunger she aroused in him. She wanted to be needed...she wanted to be loved. And that terrified her.

Because she couldn't live without him either. All along she had been playing a kind of game with him without even realising it. At no stage had she made a realistic effort to leave him. Today... That didn't count. One last-ditch attempt to do what her intelligence urged her to do, and even then she had run with the safe, sure knowledge that he would follow her. Only she hadn't dreamt that the resulting confrontation would be so cataclysmic.

Where was pride now? Rafael had smashed it, left no defence to hide behind. Her throat thickened. Quite deliberately he had employed her passionate response to him as a weapon with which to subjugate her. What price now all her angry assurances that she had no intention of marrying him? And that was exactly why he had done it. His patience had run out. Wasn't it an education to discover that when you pushed him hard enough, honour and principles simply took a hike? In a tight corner, Georgie was impulsive...but in the same position, Rafael was unrepentantly ruthless. She shivered.

His arm tightened around her. 'I would say the chances of slim to none have shortened considerably.'

Her spinal cord jerked into rigidity as his meaning sank in.

'And do you have an excuse this time?' she whispered shakily.

'None. I wanted you. I didn't give a damn.'

Georgie couldn't believe he could be that brazen. Her mouth dropped open.

'And, as you so generously assured me, a woman of your age takes responsibility for her own actions. Naturally, that freed me to be as irresponsible as I liked.'

'But you are not an irresponsible person, Rafael!' she hissed over her shoulder, very nearly giving herself whiplash, she was so indignant at having her own words thrown back at her as justification of his behaviour.

'But I'm versatile. You wouldn't believe how quickly I learn.'

She trembled with incredulous resentment. If increasing the odds of her becoming pregnant got him what he wanted, never let it be said that Rafael had shrunk from the necessity. And to think she had actually been dumb enough to believe that at the outset that frenzied lovemaking had been spontaneous on his side. Rafael? *Spontaneous*? He was a conniving, manipulative... And this was the man she loved? The anger ebbed. Yes, she did love him. Madly, passionately and probably into eternity.

She cleared her throat and took a deep breath. 'So,' she said, in what she hoped was a brisk tone. 'When's the wedding?'

He dropped the reins. Georgie twisted her head in astonishment at such clumsiness from a superb rider. The stallion had slowed to a ridiculous plodding walk anyway, without either one of them noticing, she abruptly registered. 'Rafael?'

He bent down to retrieve the reins but she caught the clenched jut of his jawline. The guy was in shock!

Georgie went white. 'Just joking,' she said in a high-pitched tone. 'You weren't really serious about marrying me... *Of course*, I guessed!' she improvised tightly. 'I just thought I'd have my revenge!'

He closed both arms round her so tightly that she could hardly breathe. 'Don't talk rubbish,' he breathed not quite steadily into her hair. 'I don't joke about things that serious.'

Plastered so close to him, she could feel the accelerated thud of his heart, the audible unevenness as he inhaled. For a split-second, when she had believed he didn't want to marry her, her entire life had metaphorically gone down a drain before her eyes and she had been ready to let the alligator snack on her, so bleak and dismal had been her future. 'I'm not sure I'm convinced,' she muttered uncertainly. 'You look shattered!'

'What an imagination you have,' he murmured, sounding reassuringly more like himself.

'You look shattered,' Georgie said again, although she had never been less keen to pursue a subject, for now that she had decided that she was going to marry him, the fear that he might have cooled off on the idea devastated her.

'Possibly I wasn't expecting you to surrender this—this...' Unusually, he hesitated.

'This quickly? This easily?' she inserted, burning with mortification. 'Expected me to be more of a challenge, did you? Suddenly discovered that when I gave you what you said you wanted, you really didn't want it at all? Well, let me tell you, I——!'

'Shut up,' Rafael snapped with a quaver in his usually level drawl. 'Because if I laugh, I'm dead in the water, *es verdad*? I'll go back to being a slimy, insensitive toerag... *Por Dios*, I have had enough of this peculiar conversation! I want to look at you...'

Impatiently anchoring his hands beneath her arms, Rafael helped her to dismount. He vaulted down in her wake and gazed at her with glittering dark eyes sharp enough to cut glass. He was perceptibly tense. Both disconcerted and confused, she looked back at him. 'Rafael, what——?' And that was as far as she got.

'Georgie, tell me truthfully—why, after all that I have done, are you prepared to marry me?'

Completely unready for so direct a question, Georgie flushed and glanced away.

'It doesn't matter what you say. It won't change anything,' Rafael stated, with a tautness at variance with the reassurance.

'You're very attractive,' she mumbled, loathing him for putting her on the hot seat without warning, miserably recalling everything he had said on the subject of marriage—emotion hadn't figured once either before or after he took her to bed and discovered she wasn't the bed-hopping tramp he had believed.

'I think we can take that as mutually understood,' Rafael retorted very drily, but with an edge of driven impatience. 'We should talk about this. Trust me and be honest. Why do you want to marry me?'

Did he suspect that she was in love with him? Did that make him feel guilty again? Did it worry him that she might be entering the marriage with expectations and demands he couldn't possibly fulfil? Slowly, Georgie lifted her fiery head, biting at her lip.

'You can give me the kind of life I've always wanted,' she answered after much frantic thought, her wide eyes eloquent of her inner turmoil.

He released his breath audibly and sent her a shimmering golden glance that was utterly impassive. '*Estupendo* . . . fine. I think I'll radio for the helicopter. You look tired,' he completed flatly.

In frustration she watched him use the radio. She took a couple of steps away. Evidently, she had said the wrong thing. But what did he want from her? She forced a stilted laugh and swung back from him. 'Rafael . . . what would you have said if I had said I wanted to marry you because I loved you?'

'I'd have laughed myself into the nearest asylum.' A sardonic smile curved his sensual mouth, hooded dark eyes gleaming over her as he threw his arrogant head back. 'And run like hell. In a marriage of—shall we say, convenience?—love would be a messy and embarrassing complication.'

He could have taken an axe to her and caused less pain. In the back of her mind she had thought that maybe in time, maybe when all the nasty ripples from the past had settled, maybe when he realised that she could make him happy, his emotions might become involved and he would contrive by some wonderful miracle to look on her as something more than a beautiful, sexually available bed-partner. But now he was telling her with brutal finality that he absolutely didn't want that kind of emotional attachment between them.

'Great . . . then we both know exactly where we stand.' With a smile a world-famous actress would have prided

herself on, Georgie concealed the fact that in one smooth
sentence he had demolished her every hope.

'And that is important,' he conceded, without any expression at all.

That seemed pretty much to take care of Rafael's desire
to talk about their future. He didn't say another word
until the helicopter landed and Georgie was too miserable and too busy hiding it to be anything other than
grateful for his silence. Exhaustion was dragging her
down by then, emotional and physical. Every bone in
her body ached. It had been the longest day of her life
and it seemed to her that she had worked through every
possible emotion in her repertoire.

'You're ready to collapse.' Taking one hard look at
her as she stumbled out of the helicopter, Rafael swept
her up into his arms and, in spite of her muffled protests, insisted on carrying her into the house.

'I think it's also important that you know that there
are times when I don't like you very much,' Georgie
whispered in a choky voice against his broad shoulder,
drinking in the familiar warm, sexy scent of him and
hating herself for being so susceptible.

'That's mutual, too.'

'You mean you don't like you or you don't like me?'
she prompted unsteadily.

'You,' Rafael supplied smoothly, as Teresa surged to
open her bedroom door.

Georgie burst into a flood of tears. She certainly
shocked him. She shocked herself even more. She hadn't
even felt the tears gathering.

'Don't be such a baby... I didn't mean it. *Madre de
Dios*,' he grated as he laid her down on the bed. 'I never
know what the hell you're likely to do next! You open
your mouth and I haven't a clue what to expect!'

'Read my lips, then,' Georgie sobbed, and mouthed
something very succinct and rude, a phrase that told him

to take himself off pronto, combined with a look that told him a jump off the balcony would be her preferred form of exit.

Rafael cast her a seething look of angry frustration. 'I think you are the most irrational woman I have ever met.'

'And s-stupid...don't forget that!' Georgie sobbed, rolling over and burying her face in the pillows, hating the way she was behaving but totally unable to suppress the need to hit out at him.

'I'm sorry.'

Her sensitive hearing suggested she was being treated to gross insincerity, an apology merely to silence her irrational exasperating behaviour.

He said it again louder, and his intonation was ice-cold.

She gulped. 'Accepted.'

'We will get married on Saturday.'

Saturday was only three days away. '*Saturday*?'

'The most convenient date in respect of my business commitments.'

Marvellous, she thought, in the mood now really to wallow in her misery. Convenient? The ceremony was to be slotted into his schedule like an appointment.

'Do you want your parents present?'

'They're on a second honeymon cruise of the Greek islands,' Georgie told him. 'Why spoil it?'

'It is your choice.' Temper back under iron wraps, he was equally dry.

Another sob snaked through Georgie. The mattress gave. 'You're overtired,' Rafael murmured tightly. 'And maybe I have seemed unsympathetic...'

Unsympathetic? What a typical Berganza understatement that was!

'This has been a very emotional day,' he persisted doggedly, impervious to the lack of encouragement he was receiving. He gripped one of her hands tightly before she could whip it under her like the other one. 'But I promise you that you will never regret marrying me. I'll make you happy... Perhaps you don't want to live here? We can live anywhere.'

Momentarily disarmed, Georgie found herself listening, quite astounded at the idea that he could be offering her a choice of where they lived when she had always believed that Rafael regarded the *estancia* as his only possible permanent home.

'Although it doesn't really matter where the bedroom is, does it?' That final softly derisive sentence swiftly put paid to any goodwill he might have reanimated.

Georgie snatched her hand away, cut to the quick. He didn't need to drive that message home any harder. She was already painfully aware of the sole value she had in his eyes. And, as the door closed behind him, Georgie wondered in an agony of doubt if once more she had foolishly allowed impulse to overrule sanity. What sort of a relationship could she possibly build with a man who regarded her in such a light?

And he had sounded bitter. What the heck did Rafael have to be bitter about? Right now, could he be feeling as confused as she did? Throughout the day, Rafael had lurched unpredictably from one mood to another. Was it conceivable that she had hit the nail squarely on the head earlier? Could it have been that, when she had finally agreed to marry him, Rafael had suddenly registerd that that really wasn't what he wanted after all?

Dear lord, how humiliating that would be... But she couldn't help remembering all that Rafael had said about the attraction of her unavailability in the past. Rafael liked a challenge. Rafael was a natural predator. For such a male, the hunt was often far more exciting than the catch. Right now, was Rafael bitterly regretting the trap he had dug for himself? Georgie simply couldn't live with that fear.

Teresa came and insisted on helping her into bed. A beautiful meal was brought up on a tray and everybody showed an embarrassing desire to fuss over her. Rafael's aunt came up to ask how she was in slow, careful English. Georgie squirmed, unhappily aware that she had caused a furore. And after that she fell asleep, waking up very late to darkness.

For a while she lay pondering her earlier misgivings, and railed at her own reluctance to face up to them. With sudden decision, she rose and pulled on her robe and tidied her hair. The lights were still on downstairs. She was aware that Rafael often worked late, being one of those individuals who seemed to thrive on little sleep.

She was on the last step of the stairs when Beatriz erupted with hot cheeks and wild eyes from Rafael's library. 'Never in my whole life have I been so insulted!' she hissed at Georgie. 'But I blame you, not Rafael. He is out of his senses with drink! What have you done to him? It is a disgrace that a man of his stature and education should be in a state of gross inebriation——'

'He's drunk?' Georgie whispered, having taken some few seconds to recognise this heaving-breasted, outraged young woman as the frigidly correct and controlled beauty she had met earlier in the day. '*Rafael*?' she stressed, almost as shattered by the idea as her companion was, but a good deal less judgemental.

'It is this ridiculous wedding... What else can it be?' Beatriz told her accusingly. 'I offered my sympathy but he was too proud to accept it. Rafael could not possibly want to marry a woman like you. You are nothing, a nobody... a social climber who used his sister as a passport into his acquaintance! Had you any decency or any respect for the name of Berganza, you would set him free!'

Leaving Georgie white and trembling in shock, Beatriz stalked up the stairs.

CHAPTER NINE

GEORGIE'S soft knock on the library door drew no response. Apprehensively, she opened the door and walked in. One light was lit on the desk. Rafael was slumped in the swivel chair behind it, his long lean legs planted on the desktop, the mess of papers there crushed indifferently by his booted feet. His face was in shadow but she could see that his eyes were closed and, surmising that he was asleep, Georgie moved closer.

He hadn't shaved for dinner, if he had had any, and hadn't changed either. His blue-shadowed jawline and tousled black hair gave him the appearance of a desperado. But the lush ebony lashes fanned down on his abrasive cheekbones were as long as a child's, and a tortured tenderness twisted through her. She didn't need Beatriz to tell her to set him free, she reflected painfully, her mouth downcurving at the sight of the low level on the bottle of malt whisky. If the prospect of marrying her reduced him to this level, Rafael could look forward to seeing the dust of her exit within hours.

And then she saw the gun lying beside the bottle. She had never seen a gun except on television. But there it was, a relatively small black metal article...a revolver? Dear God in heaven. Her stomach heaved. Rafael couldn't possibly be that desperate...could he? Anyone less likely to be contemplating suicide would be hard to find. Rafael was so strong...wasn't he? Then why was the gun there? a little voice screamed. Why, when Rafael was doing something so tremendously out of character as getting himself roaring drunk, did he suddenly have a gun sitting beside him?

Her heart in her mouth, Georgie tiptoed closer, intending to take possession of the revolver. Better safe than sorry, she decided. As she moved, a sheet of paper crunched beneath her toes, and she bent down and picked it up, intending to replace it on the desk. Her fleeting glance was caught accidentally by the lines of numerals with minus signs. Some sort of a bank statement, belonging to someone in an enormous amount of debt. Embarrassed that she had glimpsed a no doubt private document, Georgie hurriedly set it down on the desk.

'Beatriz... *vete a hacer puñetas*!' Rafael suddenly snarled.

Georgie flinched back and gasped, taken by surprise.

His lashes flew up on dark, dark eyes with a wild febrile glitter. 'What do you want?' he slurred in another tone altogether, as he visibly struggled to focus on her.

'What did you say to Beatriz to put her in such a tizzy?' Georgie asked in a falsely bright voice, to conceal her rampant nervous tension.

A sardonic smile briefly curved his taut mouth. He didn't reply.

'Rafael?' Georgie pressed worriedly.

'Leave me... I am drunk,' Rafael framed with obvious difficulty, and reached for the bottle again. '*Se acabo.*'

'What does that mean?'

Rafael surveyed her and emitted a harsh laugh. *No tengo nada... nada*!' he repeated savagely, raking her anxious face with embittered eyes which didn't seem to be quite taking her in.

I have nothing—she understood that all right. What did he mean, he had nothing? On the brink of forcing herself to ask him if it was the threat of marrying her which had prompted him to hit the bottle—and frankly, if it was, she felt more like hitting him than proffering comfort—Georgie was silenced by her confusion.

'What can I give you now?' he muttered indistinctly, tipping his glass to compressed lips.

A glimmer of devastated comprehension assailed her. Her shocked gaze suddenly stabbed back to the bank statement she had replaced on the desk. Of course, that statement belonged to him, she reasoned. Who else could it possibly belong to? He was in debt to the tune of millions. No wonder he was getting drunk!

She took a deep breath. 'Rafael...have you got business problems?'

'Business problems?' Now that did grab his full attention. His dark head fairly spun back to her, his glinting eyes narrowing intently.

'I have nothing...what can I give you now?' he had said. What else could he possibly be admitting to? She had been very slow on the uptake.

'What makes you think I might have these problems?' he contrived to enquire, looking a lot more acute and aware all of a sudden than he had a few minutes previously. He even raised himself up slightly from his slump in his seat to survey her better.

Georgie swallowed hard on the lump that had come out of nowhere into her throat. She didn't want him to think that she had been prying, so she decided not to mention having accidentally seen that damning statement. Rafael was so proud. Failure of any kind was anathema to him. Naturally he would try to cover up. But, oh, the relief of learning that his condition had nothing whatsoever to do with her or their projected marriage!

'You can be honest with me, Rafael,' she whispered tightly. 'I won't breathe a word to anyone.'

He breathed in deeply, still studying her with slightly glazed eyes. 'You think I have suffered—er—financial reverses?'

'You just told me you had!'

'I did?' Rafael pushed decidedly unsteady fingers through his black hair and seemed to be sunk in thought. Then, with startling abruptness, he glanced up again. '*Sí*,' he muttered fiercely. 'Naturally this worries you. You fear that I will not be able to supply this life of luxury you crave! And now you change your mind about marrying me, *es verdad*?'

'Rafael . . . how could you even think I would feel like that?' Georgie gasped, tears springing to her eyes, stricken for him, not for herself, because she could hardly begin to imagine what it must be like for someone like Rafael, fabulously rich all his life, suddenly to face a future deprived of the status and luxuries he no doubt took completely for granted.

'You don't think like that?' he prompted weakly, his voice just sliding away.

Georgie read that strained voice as being evidence of the depth of his despair. And she couldn't stand the distance between them any longer. Aching to offer him comfort and reassurance, she slid past the desk and threw herself on the carpet beside his chair so that she could wrap her arms round his lean waist, since she reckoned he was far too drunk to be capable of standing up. The slowness of his reactions certainly suggested that he was. As she made physical contact, he went absolutely rigid.

'Please don't push me away,' Georgie pleaded vehemently. 'Don't let your pride come between us.'

'My pride?'

'You really are drunk, aren't you?' she sighed, burying her head on his lap in a sudden surge of helpless tenderness.

'I *feel* very drunk,' Rafael confided unsteadily.

'I'll probably have to say all this again in the morning because you won't remember it. Now, listen,' she said, angling back her vibrant head with an air of stubborn determination. 'Your money has never been important to me. I don't care if you're broke or up to your ears in debt——'

'In debt?' Rafael repeated in a deeply shaken undertone.

'I suppose you don't know at this stage just how bad it's going to be, but what I'm telling you now is that it doesn't matter to me.'

'It doesn't?'

She gazed up at him, blinking back tears, absorbing only a tithe of his shattered expression through that veil of moisture. 'And I'm very hurt that you think that it could matter to me. Of course, I still want to marry you—I don't need a life of luxury to be happy.'

'You don't?'

Georgie groaned. 'I realise that you're drunk...but could you please try to stop repeating everything I say?'

A lean hand lifted and his forefinger traced the wobbling curve of her full lower lip. Instinctively, Georgie pressed her cheek into his palm and simultaneously she felt the raw tension ebb from his long, lean length. There was a long silence, violet eyes meshing mesmerically with gold.

'And do you think you could put the gun away now?'

'What gun? Oh...that one,' Rafael gathered abstractedly, with the utmost casualness. 'I must lock it away. Father Tomás learnt that it was in the possession of one of my most hot-headed *llaneros* and persuaded him to give it up before he was tempted to use it on somebody.'

Georgie's cheeks burned at the melodrama that had leapt right out of her own imagination. Rafael, still in the same uncharacteristic mood of complete relaxation, suddenly arrowed wondering dark eyes over her taut profile. '*Querida mía* . . . you surely did not think——?'

'Of course I didn't.'

'You crazy woman,' he groaned, abruptly bending down and gathering her up into a heap in his arms.

'You seem to be sobering up.'

'Shock.'

She supposed he meant the shock of the bad news he had presumably had. 'Do you want to talk about it?'

'Not tonight, *gatita*.'

She rested her head against a powerful shoulder, delighted by the reception she was receiving from him. He had been shocked that she was prepared to stand by him through thick and thin, but he had cheered up marvellously, so she was prepared to forgive him for holding so low an opinion of her.

'Your worries have been on your mind all day,' she reflected out loud, thinking of his positively insouciant manner before breakfast when he had clearly been trying to put up a macho front, and then the staggering changes of mood he had exhibited later on.

'Let us not even consider them now,' Rafael said soothingly.

She frowned. While she was no keener than he to face a presumably ghastly, stressful and horribly complex financial crisis, which was evidently destined to leave them ultimately as poor as church mice, she did feel it was something that had to be dealt with immediately. Then, what did she know about such things? What possible advice could she offer? No doubt Rafael appreciated that too and, equally certainly, he had within reach all the professional assistance he could require.

'I just wanted you to know that I'm here . . . to be supportive,' she added tautly.

'This I have noticed,' Rafael commented with a slightly dazed inflection from above her downbent head. 'After all, you are now showing some—some—er—affection for me for the very first time.'

Affection? What a milk-and-water translation of the ferociously strong feelings which were driving her! But then, she didn't want to overdo it, did she? Rafael was very proud. Very probably affection was the most he was prepared to accept until he felt in control of events again. Although she had to admit he had already made the most remarkable recovery from his apparent stupor of intoxication.

'I thought you might need it.'

'And maybe you find—er—losers more appealing?

Her head flew up. 'Rafael . . . you are not a loser,' she protested emotionally. 'Just about anybody can get into trouble with money—it doesn't mean you're a loser! You've got to allow yourself to make mistakes. Nobody's perfect.'

'I used to think I was,' Rafael breathed with sudden austerity, his stunningly handsome features hardening as his mouth curled. 'And I'm starting to realise that I got what I deserved.'

'Please . . . It depresses me to death when you start getting all grim and self-critical.'

'But I have not been sufficiently critical of my treatment of you.'

Georgie looked levelly into lustrous dark eyes. 'This is a fresh start for us. I mean, it is . . . isn't it?' she pressed, with desperate hope that this wonderful new openness she sensed between them wasn't about to prove a flash in the pan by morning. 'As if we've just met for the first time?'

'Permit me to warn you, then, that you are in serious danger of being ravished on the very first date,' Rafael murmured slumbrously, delightfully willing, it seemed, to play along with the suggestion, his hands settling on the swell of her buttocks as she sat astride him.

'It wasn't like that, though, was it? Not back then,' she remarked, unable to silence the rueful observation. 'You were so cold.'

With a stifled groan, he leant his brow against hers and sighed. 'Georgie... don't you have any idea how much restraint it took for me to keep my hands off you? I was desperate to make love to you but you were so young——'

'Was that really why?'

'I didn't want to take advantage of you and I didn't want the hunger of our bodies to take over to the exclusion of everything else... as it so easily could have done. For me, marriage is a very serious commitment which I would want to last a lifetime,' Rafael stated with firm emphasis. 'I have seen too much of the misery which broken homes inflict upon children. Think well before Saturday, *querida*. Once we are married, I will not give you your freedom again.'

Georgie felt reassured rather than challenged. At the back of her mind, she had been afraid Rafael might choose to cast her off again when familiarity bred contempt in the marital bed, as she had believed it surely would if only the most basic sexual instincts had prompted him to marry her in the first place. But now he was telling her that he expected their marriage to last.

'I need a shower and some coffee,' he said wryly. 'And you should be in bed. Beatriz will be wide awake listening for creaking floorboards, and I'm very much afraid that, if she hears them, she will take great pleasure in telling you.'

'I don't give a hoot.'

Rising up, Rafael slowly slid her to the ground. He gazed down at her and his eloquent mouth twisted. 'But I do,' he told her with quiet finality.

Georgie reddened fiercely and recognised how much had changed between them. For just a little while Rafael had seemed out of control, but now he was back in the driver's seat again, instinctively reasserting his dominance. 'I feel pretty cut off now!' she said baldly.

And he flung back his handsome head and laughed with spontaneous appreciation. It crossed her mind that he looked incredibly light-hearted for someone who was facing the loss of a fortune, said to run into billions. Was he trying to save face or something? Or were things not as bad as she had innocently imagined?

Patently unaware of her thoughts, he guided her to the door and reached for her hand. 'Georgie…that your passion matches mine is a wonderful thing,' he said intently. 'In fact, it is a source of sublime satisfaction whenever I think about it.'

He drew her to him, extracted a driving kiss that she felt sizzle right down to her toes and back up again, and then set her back again, breathing hard. *'Buenas noches, enamorada.'*

Of course, of course—he was probably intending to sober up and sit up all night and work in an effort to sort the financial mess out. It dimly occurred to her that they couldn't have picked a worse time for a wedding. Surely he would need to travel abroad and have loads of serious meetings with banks or creditors or whatever? Abruptly, Georgie said as much, before he could vanish back into the library.

Rafael stilled, black lashes swooping down low on his suddenly hooded gaze. Colour darkened his blunt cheekbones. 'No…it is absolutely essential that I maintain a pretence of normality and that no word of this leaks out before I am properly prepared to deal with it,' he stated very abruptly.

'Can you really keep the lid on something like this? Won't it make it more of a strain—sort of pile on the agony?' Georgie reasoned anxiously.

Rafael drew in a long, deep shuddering breath. A tiny muscle tugged at the corner of his unsmiling mouth. '*Querida* ... let us not spoil our wedding with such concerns,' he urged.

'Well, if you think that's best——'

'Believe me, I do.'

Biting at her lip, Georgie nodded, terribly touched that he should be putting their wedding ahead of all else. Up on the landing, she very deliberately bounced on the floorboards outside Rafael's bedroom, giggled, opened and closed the door and then crept like a mouse into her own room beside it. Her methods of dealing with Beatriz Herrera León were considerably more basic than Rafael's and nobody, least of all a nasty piece of work like the snobbish Beatriz, was about to make Georgie ashamed of the fact that she and Rafael were already lovers.

The next morning, Georgie leapt out of bed and realised how happy she was. Oddly enough, she had always scorned that old chestnut that a crisis often drew people together. If there were cracks in a relationship, the crisis was more likely to blow them wider apart. And yet look at what had happened between her and Rafael last night! Somehow all the barriers had come down between them. The hostility and the rough uneasy edges had miraculously vanished. Rafael had been really strong and tender and caring.

Anxiety flooded her as she heard the burst of voices over the breakfast-table. She was suddenly so scared that Rafael might have reverted again overnight. But the minute she entered the room, Rafael rose to greet her. With Beatriz looking on as though she was being forced to witness an indecent act, Georgie found her hand being carried to his mouth as he planted a kiss intimately to the inside of her wrist.

'You look fantastic, *querida*,' Rafael murmured in his dark, deep seductive voice while she hovered there in a haze of stunned pleasure. 'That colour is spectacular on you.'

Georgie skimmed a self-conscious hand down over her chain store-bought pink sundress and positively glowed. 'You think so?'

Hungry golden eyes clung to her vibrantly beautiful face. 'I think so.'

Georgie's gaze wandered dizzily over the open-necked white shirt and the close-fitting faded denim jeans he wore. 'You look wonderful too,' she whispered. 'I've never seen you in jeans before.'

'Your coffee is getting cold, Rafael,' Beatriz said flatly.

Beatriz discussed the price of coffee in the Third World, moved on to Bolivian politics and then did them all to death with her opinion of the British Welfare State. Absently impressed by her intelligence, Georgie ate and watched Rafael watching her and letting his coffee get cold, and she was so happy that it was like being on another planet.

'I have something for you,' Rafael informed her, pulling her chair back for her and generally behaving as though a slight draught might give her pneumonia. She loved it.

He carried her off into the drawing-room and ten seconds later he was sliding an incredibly opulent emerald ring on her engagement finger. 'Where it belongs at last.'

'You mean you bought it four years ago?' Her violet eyes swam. 'It's so *big*—I mean beautiful!' she adjusted hurriedly, biting back what he would probably consider a very tactless suggestion that, if it was as hugely expensive as it looked, he might be wiser to hang on to it and sell it.

He laughed softly, as though he could read her mind.

'Rafael?' She swallowed hard. 'I was so scared you would have changed again this morning——'

'Changed?'

'Never mind.'

'No.' Rafael tugged her slowly, indolently forward into his arms, bringing her into stirring contact with his superbly masculine body and she simply stopped breathing—she was so electrified, not only by that physical proximity but by the softened darkness of his gaze. 'From now on, I want you to share everything with me.'

'You're just so different...'

He smiled brilliantly. 'But so are you.'

That reality belatedly occurred to her. Last night, she had been all over him like a dose of chicken-pox, and this morning she had been floating around like a starstruck teenager again. And evidently he just *loved* that kind of response, she registered a little dazedly. Did it massage his ego? Was that it? Or had this miracle been solely worked by his shocked realisation that even though he had lost every penny, she was going to hang on to him like grim death?

'So I'm not going to be needing the old silver bullet again, then?' Georgie teased.

He leant forward and traced her sensitive lower lip with the tip of his tongue and she trembled, her lower limbs displaying all the solid capacity of cottonwool as a burst of heat slivered through her, swelling her breasts, pinching her tender nipples almost painfully tight. Low in her throat she moaned, and yesterday she would have been embarrassed about such instant susceptibility, but today she was ready to suggest she risked the alligator again so that they could have some privacy.

'*Por Dios,*' he whispered, in between explorations of the moist interior of her mouth which had her breathing in panting little gasps of anticipation. 'A silver bullet wouldn't stop me.'

In case she was in any doubt as to his meaning, he pressed a hand to her hip and locked her into raw connection with the hard bulge of his aroused manhood, and she grabbed at his shoulders to stay upright when every sense prompted that she lie down wantonly on the nearest available horizontal surface. He groaned in matching frustration, his big powerful body trembling against her. The knowledge that he was as close to the edge as she was made her feel incredibly proud of her femininity.

'I could come over all dizzy and go upstairs and lie down,' she whispered in desperation.

'We could saddle a couple of horses and get lost.'

'We could chuck the horses out and just go for the stables.'

'You are an incredibly sensual woman,' he muttered thickly. 'I want to be inside you again so badly...but we are going to wait for our wedding night.'

'OK.' Deciding on shock tactics, Georgie dropped her arms, eased free of his hold and strolled across the room to throw herself down on a *chaise-longue* where she extended her long tanned legs with flagrant provocation.

Incandescent golden eyes flamed over her with such a force of hunger that she ached and stopped playing. I love you, she wanted to say, I love you so much, but the awareness that that information would be seriously unwelcome silenced her. Keep it light, Georgie, keep it light, she urged herself angrily.

According to Rafael, marriage was a lifetime commitment. She had all the time in the world. The last thing she wanted to risk now was scaring him off before she got that ring on her finger. Were Rafael's emotions so disciplined that he was afraid of letting go and loving her, or had he merely been telling her up-front that while he might lust after her like mad, he just knew he wasn't capable of falling in love with her?

As he moved forward he frowned, and bent to pick up something from the carpet. 'Yours?' He extended a gold charm bracelet.

Georgie got up to accept it. 'It's always falling off. I should get the safety chain repaired.'

Rafael laughed. 'That might be a good idea.'

'Lucky it dropped off in here,' Georgie said, carefully clasping it back round her wrist. 'I'd hate to lose it. Steve gave it to me for my twenty-first——'

'Had I known, I would have dumped it in the trash.'

Georgie blinked and glanced up. Every shred of good humour had been stripped from Rafael's expression. He bristled with visible aggression, his expressive eyes cold and hard.

'Just because Steve gave it to me?' Georgie asked incredulously. 'Why are you still so hostile towards him? You know that nothing happened between us, and he is part of my family——'

'Not in my eyes, and he will never be welcome here,' Rafael asserted with grim emphasis. 'Nor will I permit you to meet him except in the company of your parents.'

Georgie was seriously tempted to giggle. It was so ridiculous. Did Rafael have any idea how ridiculous he sounded? Was he jealous? Was that the problem? Four years ago, he must have been eaten alive with sexual jealousy when he believed that Steve had been her lover and now, even though he knew what nonsense that had been, he was still stubbornly clinging to the same closed mind.

How could any sane man be jealous of a single embrace? Or was it that Rafael still suspected that she found Steve attractive, other than as a brother? Now, that idea really did worry her. If Rafael could *still* cherish such suspicions, he had a real problem. That kind of jealousy was neither amusing nor understandable...it was threatening and dangerous.

'Rafael...you know that night when Steve grabbed me and kissed me, I was really turned off,' Georgie confided. 'I do not find Steve attractive in that way——'

'I am now aware of that.'

'In fact, I was so upset and embarrassed—well, that's why I took off for Danny's for the night,' she completed.

'I have also worked this out for myself.'

'What a leap of faith that must have taken!' Georgie couldn't help her sarcasm. Her explanations had not altered Rafael's attitude one iota. Freezing austerity still stamped his set, dark features. 'I'm rather glad I've lost touch with poor Danny.'

'He was merely a friend. Naturally I accept that now——'

'But not my stepbrother, who is my brother in all but blood?'

Rafael sent her a smouldering look. 'I do not wish to discuss this matter further.'

Georgie tussled with her hot temper as Rafael banded an arm round her narrow back. 'We have so many other things more important to discuss,' he reminded her.

Instantly, Georgie was cooled and stabbed by conscience. Why on earth was she wittering on about Steve when she knew that Rafael was under great strain? Now was not the time to tell him that he was being unreasonable. 'I'm sorry,' she sighed. 'You must be really worried.'

Ebony lashes lifted on golden eyes. 'About what? Oh...*that*!' he grasped, contriving to look suddenly very grave again as his arm dropped from her. 'But didn't we agree that we would forget about that until after the wedding?'

'Yes, but——'

'No buts.'

'You must have nerves of steel. The way you've been behaving, nobody would even suspect that there's anything wrong.'

'It is in the back of my mind constantly,' Rafael sighed heavily. 'But I am depending on you to help me to be strong.'

He was standing over by the window, his back turned to her as if he couldn't quite bring himself to make such a demand and look her in the face. Georgie took the hint and closed her arms round him. He swivelled fluidly and pressed her face into the hard wall of his chest. A tremor ran through him. 'Let's get some fresh air,' he suggested.

It was a wonderful day. He showed her round the estancia, introduced her to everyone and made up ridiculous stories about all his illustrious but deeply boring-looking ancestors that had her falling about in hysterics. She had forgotten what a wonderful sense of humour Rafael had when he let his guard down. They spent the afternoon in the swimming-pool, and were still sitting talking at the dinner table long after Tía and Beatriz had excused themselves to go to bed. And even though Georgie slept alone, she slept like a log.

The second day was even better. The helicopter dropped them at the mouth of the Rio Tuichi, where they were met by a guide and a motorised canoe, and they cruised through a section of rainforest until it was time to go back, and Georgie wasn't a bit sorry that Rafael was lowering himself to a simple tourist excursion for her benefit. She was well aware that he usually travelled into the Amazon with various professionals in tow and camped out to rendezvous with Indians from the more remote settlements. She was equally aware just how much pleasure he was receiving from showing her a world she had never dreamt of sharing with him.

She went up to her room to change for dinner and was stunned to find the closets and cabinets in the dressing-room, stuffed full of unfamiliar garments. Bewildered, she fingered a shot silk top and palazzo pants outfit with a famous designer label.

'Like them?' Rafael grinned at her stunned expression from the doorway. She hadn't even heard him enter her bedroom.

'Everything is in my size.'

'It's yours. I had a selection ordered. Exquisite as you look in that white dress you wear every night for dinner, I thought you might enjoy a change.'

'But these kind of clothes cost a fortune!' Georgie gasped. 'And I thought you were broke!'

Rafael winced and actually paled. 'Things aren't quite as bad as that—not as bad as I initially imagined, that is,' he added, studying her frowning, surprised face intently.

'They aren't? Are you sure?' Georgie persisted in considerable confusion. 'Why didn't you say?'

'I was about to... Wear that for dinner,' he suggested in an intimate tone that quite sent her temperature rocketing and blitzed her reasoning powers. 'Turquoise and green will look stupendous with your hair, *querida mía*.'

Georgie threaded a self-conscious hand through her torrent of curls and smiled blissfully at him. 'You think so?'

'I think so.'

'Will you be able to keep your jet?'

Rafael's lustrous gaze narrowed. '*Perdón*?'

'I just couldn't picture you travelling economy class,' she confided.

He lounged back against the door-lintel and treated her to a devastating smile. 'I do believe that I will be able to save you from such a sight.'

The third day, the day before the wedding, Georgie went out riding with Rafael. When they returned to the house, Rafael was called to the phone, and she found herself seated alone with Beatriz, Tía having opted for breakfast in bed.

'You must be pregnant,' Beatriz said coldly, right out of the blue. 'Why else would he be marrying you?'

Georgie stiffened. 'I am not pregnant.'

'I was betrothed to Rafael as a child,' Beatriz told her with icy dignity.

'I'd be a liar if I said I was sorry it didn't work out,' Georgie managed after a long pause, belatedly registering why the brunette disliked her so intensely. She had been far too wrapped up in her own happiness to spare more than the most fleeting thought for Beatriz, who was the most snobbish, moralising bore she had ever met. The other woman was also beautiful, highly intelligent and very accomplished, she had to concede in all fairness, although it went against the grain to do so.

'His father died, and then mine. He would have married me had he not met *you*,' Beatriz said thinly. 'And I want you to know, before you congratulate yourself on your success on trapping him, that I intend to tell Rafael that your arrival in our country during his sister's absence was no accident.'

'I beg your pardon?'

'The whole family knows. It was a standing joke. Every time María Cristina made it known that she had issued another invitation for you to visit, she left the country soon afterwards!'

'Say that again,' Georgie invited breathlessly.

'She confided in Tía. That is how I know. In her innocence, María Cristina wanted to bring you and Rafael together, and obviously you persuaded her to do it!'

'Then how do you explain the fact that I didn't come to her wedding?' Georgie was in a daze, but a great whoop of laughter was mingling with her incredulity.

All these years she had believed that her best friend was entirely ignorant of her feelings for Rafael. But María Cristina had clearly known all along and kept quiet, perhaps out of respect for Georgie's apparent wish for privacy. And, in her own uniquely scatty way, María Cristina had tried to throw them together... by ensuring that if ever Georgie did arrive in Bolivia she would find herself stranded and forced to contact Rafael.

'And I was so very disappointed when you failed to show...'

Both female heads spun. Rafael was poised several feet inside the door, a curious half-smile playing at the corners of his sensual mouth as he looked at Georgie. 'Did you know that María Cristina knew about us?'

'But does she? Or was it just me—I mean my feelings—she guessed at?' Georgie stumbled awkwardly. 'I never told her anything!'

'Neither did I.'

'You don't understand, Rafael,' Beatriz put in with distaste. 'The woman you are on the brink of marrying plotted and planned to throw herself in your path——'

'How flattering,' Rafael drawled.

'And, what is worse, she manipulated María Cristina into doing her bidding.'

'My sister has the temperament of a mule,' Rafael said drily. 'I don't think anybody has ever manipulated her into doing anything she didn't want to do.' He switched smoothly to Spanish and, a moment later, Beatriz went puce, stood up, stalked out and left them alone.

'She said you were betrothed as children.'

'Our fathers certainly discussed it, but she was only a child at the time and there was no formal betrothal. However, when I remained single, Beatriz began to nurture certain ambitions,' he volunteered. 'She has a keen sense of her own many virtues and will undoubtedly make someone a splendid wife, but she lacks any sense of humour and, between you and me, I would as soon take a refrigerator to bed!'

A startled giggle erupted from Georgie, and then her face tightened worriedly as she searched his. 'I didn't do what she said . . . and I can't believe that María Cristina deliberately invited me here, knowing she would be abroad.'

'If my sister did, I should be very angry. To strand a young woman in a foreign country where she does not even speak the language is not a joke.'

'All the same, I think I could forgive her.'

'You may amuse yourself ferreting out the truth when she arrives this evening.'

'María Cristina's coming *tonight*?' Georgie flew to her feet. 'And I haven't even told her—I didn't even ask you for her phone number!'

'She doesn't know about the wedding. I swore Antonio to silence,' Rafael admitted mockingly. 'She doesn't even know you're here.'

'I really can't believe we're getting married tomorrow,' Georgie confided helplessly.

'What could possibly go wrong now?' Encircling her with his arms, Rafael eased her close and, briefly, she rested her cheek against his shoulder, drinking in the scent and feel of him.

'I'm not sure I can handle being so happy,' Georgie whispered unsteadily.

'Are you happy?' Narrowed dark eyes roamed over her upturned face. 'Is the past finally behind us?'

Georgie shrugged playfully, her fingers flirting with his silk tie and lingering to splay against the muscular breadth of his chest. 'What past?'

A lean hand clamped over hers, his gaze turning incandescent gold with hunger, his expressive mouth curling with amusement. 'I've been wondering...where did you pick up those moves you unleashed on me that night in the Ferrari?'

Georgie reddened. 'Magazines.'

He looked down at her for a stunned instant. 'What sort of magazines?'

'Perfectly respectable women's magazines...' Georgie shifted sinuously against him, eased her free hand below his silk-lined jacket and skimmed her fingers along his waistline, feeling the muscles in his flat hard stomach jerk tight in involuntary response. 'And you know something, Rafael...it was all true. You reacted like a textbook case and then you blew it,' she sighed.

'The next time you do that I want you to...' And as he bent his dark head down and told her in explicit language exactly what he wanted her to do next, she went hot all over and weak at the knees.

When his mobile phone buzzed and took him off to the library, Georgie felt bereft. She also felt a little embarrassed for herself. Every time she got within hailing distance of him, she behaved like a wanton. The intense sexual attraction between them just took over, but she couldn't help being aware that Rafael's control was far stronger than hers. Maybe she should be playing it more coolly. If she didn't, Rafael was likely to tumble shrewdly to the fact that she simply couldn't keep her hands off him because she loved him and that was the only way she had of expressing those feelings.

In the late afternoon, she was fixing flowers in the hall, cheerfully unconcerned by the knowledge that she had no hope of matching Beatriz's magnificent arrangement in the drawing-room. When she heard the helicopter flying in low, she didn't even lift her head. Helicopters came and went on a regular basis on the *estancia*. About five minutes later, however, Teresa came rushing in from outside. 'Your brother has come, *señorita*!' she gasped, out of breath. 'I not expect, nobody tell me he was coming. Where do I put a brother to sleep——?'

'*Steve*? Steve's here?' Georgie interrupted in astonishment, the flower she had in her hand dropping unnoticed to the polished floor.

CHAPTER TEN

GEORGIE flew across the gardens and sighted Steve's familiar, broadly built figure, the sun glinting on his thatch of blond hair. A delighted smile lit up her features as she raced up to him. 'How on earth did you know where I was?' she demanded.

Steve studied her with a tight mouth. He looked pale and strained, almost as though he had been bracing himself for a far less welcoming reception. 'I received a call from our mutual parents.'

'But I haven't been in touch with them——'

'Berganza is having them whisked off their ship and flown out here for the wedding, I believe.'

'Gosh…he thinks of everything, doesn't he?' Georgie shook her head slowly. 'I didn't like to mention them coming because I thought I'd left it too late. He must want to surprise me.'

'How sweet of him,' Steve sneered, his pale blue eyes cold with condemnation. 'Thanks for telling me you were getting married. You came out here just to run after him, didn't you? You never let on to a soul what you were planning!'

'Because I didn't *plan* it! It just happened,' Georgie muttered, taken aback by the attack. 'And OK, I know you don't like him but, for my sake, surely you can grit your teeth and be pleasant?'

'I'm hoping to take you back home with me.'

'No chance. I love him,' Georgie said baldly. 'Please don't spoil things, Steve.'

'You've been out here...what? A week? And you're marrying him? Have you lost your mind? Have you forgotten what he did to you the last time?'

'There was a misunderstanding which I don't want to go into,' Georgie said awkwardly. 'And I appreciate that you think I'm jumping in feet first, but maybe you should know that Rafael was going to ask me to marry him back then——'

'Like hell he was!'

'You haven't seen the mermaid taps.' For a moment, Georgie looked positively smug.

'I don't know what the blazes you're talking about and, to be blunt, I don't care! I'm taking you back to London with me right now.' A large hand clamped round her slender forearm.

Georgie gazed up at her stepbrother in disbelief. 'Have you gone mad? I'm getting married tomorrow.'

'He'd make you bloody miserable. He's a womaniser, Georgie. If he's willing to give you a ring, it's only because that's the only way he can get you!' Steve said unpleasantly.

'Don't be stupid... Look, what's the matter with you?' Georgie shot at him with shocked eyes. 'Why are you acting like this?'

'Get your hands off her.'

Georgie's head spun. Rafael was standing about ten feet away, both fists clenched. He wore an expression of chilling menace. 'Oh, no, don't you start,' she snapped in exasperation. 'What is the matter with the two of you?'

'You were safe,' Rafael drawled at Steve, his golden features set with blistering derision. 'You were safe, though you didn't know it. I had no intention of telling her.'

'Telling me what?' Georgie broke in, as Steve's fingers loosened their grip and finally dropped from her. She stepped back from him, her head spinning between the two men, both of whom were ignoring her. Steve was rigid and pale, breathing heavily. Rafael had an aura of violence she had never seen in him before. It scared her. Although the two men were fairly evenly matched in size, she sensed that Rafael had a killer instinct which Steve lacked. And she also knew, after one shocked glance at Rafael's shimmering golden gaze, that he had every intention of getting physical.

'Right,' she said, raising her hands in what she hoped was a strong, meaningful motion. 'I am not having this. If you lay one finger on him, Rafael . . . the wedding is off. Steve may be behaving like an idiot but you are not helping matters, and I would like him all in one piece for the photos——'

'You think I'm scared of that slimy bastard?' Steve seethed, striding forward and thrusting her roughly out of his path.

'Go back to the house, *querida*,' Rafael murmured in a flat aside.

Georgie shook her head vehemently. 'No way!'

'If you do not go voluntarily, I will have my bodyguards carry you back,' Rafael told her, with a sudden spurt of flaming impatience.

'Did you hear me tell you that I'm not marrying you if you touch him?' Georgie's voice wobbled with rage and pain. The threat hadn't made Rafael bat a magnificent eyelash.

'It's your word against mine, Berganza! Who do you think she'll believe?' Steve slung aggressively. 'There's a lot of family mileage in twenty-one years. Are you going to take that risk?'

'Oh, beat the hell out of each other...I'm past caring!' Georgie hissed at the pair of them in disgust, stalking off several yards, hoping that her stinging scorn would cool Rafael off. She just couldn't believe that he was behaving like this. And what were they talking about? Steve's word against Rafael's on *what*?

She glanced back over her shoulder before she realised that Rafael had actually taken her at her word. Appalled, she watched him take a swing at Steve. Her stomach clenched with nausea as the blow connected. 'Stop that . . . right now!' she shrieked, and began racing back, ready to throw herself between them, but someone caught her from behind, anchoring a restraining arm round her.

'What the——?' Craning her neck, she discovered one of Rafael's bodyguards gazing down at her with a mixture of embarrassment, apology and steel determination to do as he had evidently been told.

Georgie actually thought she was going to be sick when she saw Rafael hitting Steve again. She had never realised that the sight of two men fighting could be so brutal or so frightening. And she had been right in her estimation of the odds. Her stepbrother was on the brink of being hammered to a pulp and there was absolutely nothing she could do to stop it. Nobody was about to interfere.

'I'll never forgive you,' she screamed at Rafael, and she really meant it. The man was an animal. She didn't care what lay between the two men, could not imagine that there could be anything capable of excusing the savagery being enacted before her. And she was devastated that Rafael could behave in such a fashion. She saw her hopes and her dreams breaking into pieces in front of her. Seeing this side of Rafael terrified her. He was a maniac, subject to paranoid jealousy—that was all she could think.

Steve hit the ground and stayed down. Was he unconscious? Rafael spun on his heel and walked away, pausing with apparent calm to address some instruction to one of the hovering men, who had been watching the fight. The arm round Georgie dropped away. She sped over to Steve. He was already lifting his head with a groan.

'God...' he mumbled, wiping the blood away from his mouth. 'I hate to admit it but I'm glad you stayed. I think he'd have killed me if he hadn't had you as an audience.'

'The doctor will see to him,' Rafael murmured icily from behind her.

'The only person who needs a doctor around here is you!' Georgie gasped in quivering disgust. 'A psychiatrist! Tell Teresa to pack my clothes—*my* clothes, not those fancy rags you bought. I'm not going back into that house. I am not marrying you. And I never want to hear from you again...is that clear?'

Rafael raked diamond-hard dark eyes from Georgie's furious face down to Steve's emerging look of relief. He released his breath in a soft hiss. Four centuries of icy hauteur tautened his proud dark features. 'The loser takes all, *es verdad*? You take his side over mine...'

'It's one heck of a lot more complex than that!' Georgie vented not quite steadily, but she met his eyes in a head-on collision.

'But you are the woman I intended to marry and you have neither loyalty nor trust in me,' Rafael condemned.

'This is so painfully melodramatic,' Steve said snidely, picking himself up.

Rafael hit him again.

Georgie just couldn't believe it. Her stepbrother went sprawling back on the ground again, clutching his nose and groaning.

'Go with him. I no longer want you,' Rafael delivered. 'But you deserve to know the truth before you leave.'

'What truth?'

Rafael stared down at Steve's prone figure with burning loathing and contempt. 'Have you the guts to tell her, or must I do that as well?' As the taut silence stretched and her stepbrother made no response, Rafael emitted a harsh laugh. 'He was in love with you four years ago——'

'*No!*' Georgie interrupted sharply.

'And you rejected him that night. He was jealous and he was bitter,' Rafael continued in the same murderously quiet drawl. 'And when I came looking for you the next morning, he *confessed* all to me, but he confessed to lies. He told me you had been lovers since you were seventeen, that he loved you and wanted to marry you——'

Georgie started to tremble, her darkened violet eyes clinging to Steve's clenched profile. 'No, he couldn't have done that...'

'He was very convincing. He even told me how ashamed he was of taking advantage of your youth and inexperience, but that he just couldn't help himself!' Rafael spelt out in disgust.

A stifled sound of distress broke from Georgie. Suddenly she knew that she was hearing the truth. Steve couldn't even meet her eyes, nor was he making any attempt to defend himself. She was appalled.

'And, not content with that, he suggested that you had also slept with your friend Danny, and he told me how much he blamed himself for damaging your ability to tell the difference between real love and sexual pleasure!' Rafael completed witheringly.

'You couldn't have done that to me,' Georgie whispered sickly, staring at Steve.

'Wake up, Georgie. He did it because, as far as he was concerned, if he couldn't have you, he didn't want me to have you either!' Rafael scorned. 'Your rejection of him must have cut deep indeed. This man, who stood in the position of a brother to you—he thought nothing of voicing filthy foul lies which resulted in your pain and humiliation. I assume that was your punishment for not finding him attractive... and mine was having my faith and my trust in the woman I loved totally destroyed! Never would I have believed that a man who was a member of your family, who had watched you grow up and behaved as a brother towards you, could have stooped to such a level as he did. Or that any man would confess *falsely* to such shameful behaviour!'

Georgie was in deep shock, her anguished eyes clinging to Rafael's dark, driven features. She was appalled that she had never once suspected that Steve could have been in love with her then. Yet she dimly understood how fixed an image one could form of a family member, how easy it could be never to question what might lie behind that safe image. She had been very close to Steve but, in the absence of any form of sexual awareness on her side, she had been effectively blind to his feelings, translating his interest and concern for her as purely brotherly responses. Only now did she see so clearly that Steve had been too interested and too concerned... and too hostile towards Rafael.

'It's all behind us now, for God's sake,' Steve muttered heavily.

'But you came here to take her away sooner than risk exposure. You didn't want her to know the truth,' Rafael asserted. 'And I was fool enough to keep quiet because I didn't want to hurt her.'

Georgie flinched and covered her hot face with cold, trembling hands. 'I didn't know... how could I have?'

But, looking back, she saw Steve at her shoulder playing devil's advocate, stirring the pot of her insecurity about Rafael, undermining their relationship at every opportunity by planting little darts where they would cause the most damage. She also grasped the full extent of Steve's deception, shuddered as she recalled his sympathetic response to Rafael's rejection of her.

'How could you do that to me? You knew I loved him!' Georgie burst out abruptly, and then she noticed that Rafael had already walked away, that she was alone with her stepbrother.

'I thought you'd get over him, maybe turn to me.' Steve rose upright, dug his hands into his pockets and looked back at her with rueful eyes. 'I had it bad. It was a long time before I accepted that I was beating my head up against a brick wall and that you were never going to feel the same way.'

'But to tell him *that*——' In distress she turned away.

'He didn't have to believe it,' Steve said defensively.

But Georgie understood exactly why Rafael had believed those lies. Rafael was fundamentally a very honourable man. He had known that Steve loved her, seen them kiss, been forced to witness her close ties with her stepbrother. No, she didn't blame Rafael for believing, she blamed herself for being so bound up in her love that she had been blind to what was happening around her. And ironically, four years ago, Rafael had actually protected Steve by choosing not to face her with what he had been told. Why?

Why had he continued to protect her from the truth about Steve? Rafael had known how much the truth would hurt, and hurt it had and did, but perhaps not to the degree which Rafael had assumed. The intervening years had eroded her close ties with her stepbrother.

'I'm sorry,' Steve said. 'I just couldn't face it coming out. I got over you. It's behind me——'

'But you still didn't want me to be with him——'

'I'm never going to like the guy, Georgie. What do you expect? What do you think it was like for me standing by on the sidelines watching the two of you together?' he asked with remembered bitterness. 'I'm not proud of what I did, but I didn't think he had any intention of marrying you. He put the weapon in my hand when he told me he'd seen us kissing, and I'm sorry, but I couldn't resist using it.'

Dully she nodded, for she could dimly understand that.

'Look... I'm off. I'd be distinctly *de trop* at the wedding,' Steve muttered with a grim smile. 'Maybe I'll make it for the first christening... OK?'

'There isn't going to be a wedding,' Georgie reminded him in a shaky voice.

Making his stiff and painful passage back towards the helicopter he had arrived in, Steve turned his head. 'Georgie...the fight was a *male* thing, if you know what I mean, and you shouldn't have interfered.'

'It was disgusting!'

'But oddly enough I feel better.' Steve grimaced at her look of disbelief. 'It's like it's finally finished now and, since I'm feeling generous, I'll give you another reason why he took until now to tell you what I did... and why he just walked away. I think he's scared.'

'Scared? Rafael?' Georgie parroted.

'Scared that once you knew how I used to feel about you, that fondness you *once* had for me,' he explained wryly, 'might just warm up into something more meaningful.'

Georgie froze, and turned an abstracted glance on him as he headed for his transport out. But all she had sought to do was stop the fight, naturally not wanting to see the two men come to blows. Then, she hadn't known just how powerful a motivation lay behind Rafael's need for physical vengeance. And then, afterwards, Rafael had said, 'The loser takes all,' when she had rushed to Steve's aid, believing Rafael to be the main aggressor and therefore underserving of her attention. Maybe she should have kicked Steve while he was down, she thought hysterically. In Rafael's presence she had not condemned what Steve had done... she had still been too shocked.

She hurried back to the house and was shattered to discover Teresa in her bedroom, laying out her clothes on the bed to pack them.

Teresa sighed, and shook her head. 'Ees very hard to understand this on, off, on, off wedding.'

Her heart in her throat, Georgie ran Rafael to earth in the drawing-room where he was standing moodily surveying an ancestral portrait with a large drink in one hand.

'Oops...gosh...I didn't think what I was saying when I said the wedding was off.' Georgie leapt in and tested the water straight off.

'I will put no pressure on you to remain,' Rafael retorted harshly.

'All right, if that's the way you feel about it...' Georgie drew herself up to her full height, her chin tilting, and then drew in a deep, shivering breath. 'Well, actually, it's not all right because I'm not going—not unless you tell me that you want me to go.'

'You have your mind of your own.' Hooded dark eyes flicked her a forbidding glance. 'Where is he now?'

'Steve? Probably airborne by now. He reckoned he would be unwelcome at the wedding but he might just make it for the first christening,' Georgie dared.

Rafael's jawline clenched. 'I forgot about that possibility.'

'Fancy that, and just a few days ago, that was all you could think about!' Georgie reminded him helplessly.

'No doubt that is why you insist that you are not leaving,' he drawled in the same unyielding tone.

'Franky, no. Whether or not I might be pregnant hasn't even crossed my mind and it wouldn't influence my feelings either way,' Georgie stated with perfect truth. 'It isn't a good enough reason to get married.'

'Then what have we to discuss?'

Georgie went white. Steeling herself, she had been trying to work up to telling him how she really felt about him. No more lies, no more half-truths to save face, she had told herself, no more room for misunderstandings. Pride urged her to agree the point and go with dignity, as she had not done four long years ago. But now she knew that, then, Rafael had undoubtedly been far kinder to her than most men would have been in the same situation. He had not thrown Steve's sordid revelations in her face and she still marvelled at that restraint.

'Rafael...I am very sorry that Steve lied like that——'

'It is not your place to apologise for him...or is it?' he growled, glittering golden eyes on her with almost physical force. 'Do you now defend him for what he did, even though it was your reputation he destroyed?'

'No...I don't defend him at all. I think it was a revolting thing to do and I was very shocked, but it happened four years ago,' Georgie stressed tautly, her violet eyes clinging to his hard, set features. 'And I can't get as worked up about it as you can because I didn't know about it when it really mattered. I also thought that we had overcome the past...but it seems I was wrong!'

'Your sole concern was for him out there——'

'And you've accused *me* of being childish,' Georgie suddenly launched at him, her voice nonetheless shrill with distress, for she wasn't getting through to Rafael. He had withdrawn to some remote place, outraged and offended. 'That was before I knew what you were fighting about and I thought Steve had been knocked out. You hate him and I can understand that now——'

'How can you understand what I feel? How can you possibly understand?' Rafael suddenly shot at her in savage surge. 'Thanks to him, I lost the woman I loved four years ago and, thanks to him, I have lost you again!'

'You haven't lost me.' Georgie licked her dry lips.

'I do not want you without love. It wouldn't work.' Rafael stared down broodingly into his half-empty glass, his strong features strikingly taut. 'I am already bitter— how much more bitter would I become, thinking of what we once had and lost? I cannot pretend that what we have is enough, when I would always be wanting what you could not give me,' he bit out with raw emotion. 'So, go while I am in this sane state. I do not want a broken marriage between us and I see no way of us ever overcoming the past.'

Sentenced to stillness by the savage edge to his emotional delivery, Georgie was afraid in that welter of bitter words, she had somehow misinterpreted what she had heard. Her heartbeat was racing madly behind her ribcage. 'Rafael,' she said weakly.

'I feel resentment now, even though I have no entitlement to it,' Rafael continued darkly. 'You were the victim, not I. It was not you who lied, not you who were stupid enough to swallow his lies, and I was the one who walked away, so what right do I now have to demand more than you are capable of feeling? You desire me, and you have a naturally sunny and affectionate disposition and, for many men, that would be enough. But is is not enough for me. If I cannot have it all, I am better off with nothing.'

Tears swam in her eyes and she wrinkled her nose to hold them at bay. She had never seen him so worked up and, characteristically, he was looking solely on the dark side, apparently unable even to consider the idea that she might, after all, be capable of giving him what he insisted he needed. She cleared her throat. 'Are we talking about love?'

His beautifully shaped mouth tightened and she realised that pride had permitted him to talk all the way round the subject as long as the fatal word was not actually mentioned. 'What else?'

A surge of joy filtered through Georgie, restoring the colour to her cheeks, chasing off the strain from her vibrant face. 'Oh, well, if that's all, you've been unusually modest in your assumptions. And I would have said you were not the modest type——'

'What are you talking about?' Rafael demanded, with no diminution in his grim bearing.

'Let me give you this scenario, Rafael. You spirit me out here with the worst of gothic intentions. How hard did I try to escape? Why did I go to bed with you? Why did I finally agree to marry you? Why was I prepared to stay with you even though you might lose everything?' Georgie questioned with a helpless smile, although she had intended to keep him hanging to the end. 'And, if you're as clever as I think, you ought to be coming to one of two possible conclusions. Either I'm as limp as a wet dishcloth or I'm crazy about you.'

'*Es verdad?*' Rafael searched her bright, speaking eyes and suddenly dropped the cold front. He strode forward and gripped her shoulders. 'You are serious?'

'I'm beginning to think I never really stopped being crazy about you. I love you so much... How can you not see that?' she whispered ruefully.

'I didn't. I thought you felt sorry for me when you saw me getting drunk, and I was prepared to use that to hold you,' he confessed, a dark flush accentuating his handsome cheekbones. 'But it was a shameful thing to do.'

No, it had been an education, but she was tactful enough to keep that acknowledgement to herself. 'You were that desperate?' she couldn't help prompting.

'I wanted what we had back and I believed it was lost forever... but it was not lost for me,' Rafael muttered, with something less than his usual perfect English. 'You had not been here very long before I understood that even with all the unpleasant things I had believed of you, I still loved you.'

'You love me too?' Georgie was in seventh heaven.

'It was not only the desire which tore my heart out from the first day,' Rafael told her with satisfying fervour as he pulled her up against him and stared down at her with adoring dark eyes and a slightly stunned expression, as if he still couldn't yet believe that she loved him back. 'It was the liking and the laughing too. Your spirit, your sense of humour, the manner in which you stood up to me. I had turned you into a shallow bitch inside my mind over the years, and then instantly I was faced with the reality that, whatever your morals were, you were really still the warm, vibrant girl I fell in love with at the age of seventeen——'

'I love the sound of your voice,' Georgie confided honestly, 'especially when you're saying things like that. Did you really fall for me back then?'

'One look that first day and it was like being hit by lightning.'

'Lightning struck twice. I thought you were gorgeous. I couldn't take my eyes off you,' Georgie admitted unsteadily.

'*Te quiero, querida mía.*' Tired of talking, Rafael raked impassioned eyes over her and lifted her up in his arms to devour her mouth with an intense hunger he no longer tried to hide.

Some timeless minutes later, Georgie registered that what she was lying on was not a bed, but a rigid and hard sofa. Rafael's jacket was on the floor along with his tie, and his shirt was hanging open, revealing the glorious expanse of his muscular chest. She scratched her fingernails through the curling dark hair hazing his pectorals, smiling a very feminine smile of power as he shuddered in response and came back down to her again fast, sealing his hard body to hers in a movement that gave her no doubt of his ultimate intentions.

'You are wearing too many clothes,' he muttered raggedly, positively aflame with impatience.

'I thought we were waiting for tomorrow night,' Georgie gasped, as one lean hand closed over the mound of one swelling breast, frustratingly barred from him by the tight bodice of her fitted top.

'Forget that,' Rafael groaned. 'I cannot wait...'

'And to think I thought you were not a spontaneous guy,' Georgie sighed in delight.

Neither one of them heard the door open. They were far too busy kissing.

'Tía's no great shakes as a chaperon, is she?'

Rafael's head flew up in shock. Georgie froze. As Rafael sprang off the sofa, Georgie sat up and grinned from ear to ear. María Cristina was wearing a matching grin on her rounded, pretty face.

'This is going to take a lot of living down, brother dear,' Rafael's sister asserted, tickled pink at having surprised her very self-disciplined older brother in such a situation. 'And in the drawing-room too, where anybody could walk in.'

'Anybody else would have had the good manners to knock,' Rafael vented in a driven undertone.

Georgie flew across the room into her friend's arms. 'You already knew I was here!'

'I knew the day you arrived. I've been in cahoots with Teresa. I swear it was excitement which sent me into labour,' María Cristina chuckled. 'Go and meet your nephew, George,' she said to Rafael. 'Georgie and I have some catching up to do.'

Teresa brought coffee. Antonio, María Cristina's husband, wandered in briefly to be introduced. Teresa brought Georgie's namesake in and he was much admired before he closed his big dark eyes and went cheerfully back to sleep in his beribboned Moses basket.

'Of course I knew you were in love with my brother,' her friend laughed. 'And I thought he was in love with you. I even guessed when you started seeing each other. Rafael was so happy and you floated about as if you were on a cloud. Then you broke up, and ever since I've been racking my brains on how to bring the two of you together again. This time, when I invited you, I was really devious and I took an awful risk——'

'You knew you were going to California and yet you practically pleaded with me to come and stay with you?'

'Guilty... but it worked. You had to contact Rafael to find out where I was, and I knew he was still interested because he was always so keen to know what you said in your letters and what you were doing,' María Cristina confided. 'But I have to tell you, with a wedding arranged for tomorrow, the pair of you have more than exceeded my wildest expectations!'

'Are you pleased?'

'Georgie, I'm over the moon! I couldn't be more delighted—Rafael has been so gruesomely serious since you broke up...'

'Alone at last,' Rafael groaned, leaning back against the door as he locked it. *Por Dios*...what are you wearing?'

Sinuously sheathed in a peach satin and lace teddy, which made no attempt to pretend that its function was anything but pure female provocation, Georgie lounged back against the pillows on the comfortable bed and shamelessly basked in the reality that her new husband was riveted by the view.

They had had the most glorious wedding-day, with her parents and all Rafael's closest relatives in attendance. Georgie thought headily of the moment Rafael had slid that gold ring on her finger and of the expression of love in his rich dark eyes. Her toes curled, just reliving that moment of knowing that she was the most wonderful woman in the world as far as he was concerned.

'You haven't even asked where we are going,' Rafael said mockingly, dropping his jacket in a careless heap and coming down on the bed beside her.

Her heart raced at his proximity. The throb of the jet engines was not as loud as her own heartbeat. 'I'm expecting to be taken to heaven tonight,' she whispered, running wantonly possessive eyes over his magnificent length.

'I have the villa in the Caribbean.'

'I can't wait that long...'

Rafael leant down and extracted a devastatingly erotic kiss that turned her bones to liquid honey. 'Did you think I would ask you to?'

She linked her arms round his brown neck, weak with longing. Golden eyes merged with violet in the smouldering silence.

'*Te quiero, enamorada,*' he muttered feverishly, and drew her close. For a long time afterwards there was nothing but the heated rise of their breathing and her long, gasping sighs of pleasure. Satiated, they lay wrapped tightly together in an intimate tangle of limbs.

'I'm glad you didn't have to get rid of the jet. This bed is very convenient,' Georgie sighed.

Rafael tautened. 'I have a confession to make.'

'Anything bar murder, you're forgiven,' Georgie mused dizzily, running a worshipping hand over his smooth golden back.

'I lied about the financial reverses...'

'You *lied*?' Forcing him back from her, Georgie sat up and surveyed him in horror and bewilderment. 'But how could you have been lying? I saw a bank statement lying on the floor that night, and it must have belonged to you, and the account was in the red to the tune of six figures.'

'A bank statement?' Rafael frowned. 'In the red ... Ah, those statements I was studying that night belonged to a bankrupt company I was thinking of buying.'

'Really?' Feeling decidedly foolish, Georgie went very pink and dropped that angle. 'You were saying that you lied to me, which I consider quite unforgivable!'

Rafael started talking fast. 'But you warmed to me as never before when you thought I was having business problems,' he protested.

'You rat, you utter rat!' Georgie screeched at him, reflecting on her painful enactment of the stand-by-your-man routine.

'Think of our children ... you would not want them to be poor, surely?' Rafael reasoned in desperation.

'You must have been laughing your socks off at me that night!'

'No, for the first time I was encouraged to hope that I could win you back,' Rafael asserted. 'So I thought maybe I would be a loser for a little while and see what happened——'

'You played on my sympathy, you sneaky, conniving rat,' Georgie condemned afresh. 'What was all that guff about you having nothing left?'

'Without your love, I had nothing. That was why I was drowning my sorrows and feeling sorry for myself. You had told me you wanted me only for the life I could give you, and that cut deep...'

'You deserved it—all that posturing about love being messy and complicating things. That was your pride talking.'

'*Sí...*'

'Without your love, I had nothing.' And he really meant it. 'Maybe I can forgive you this once,' she sniffed, not surrendering too easily and keeping her distance. 'On the other hand, I could walk out...'

'We are sixty thousand feet above the ground.' As he made the reminder his striking features were slashed with helpless amusement. 'Not that I would expect a small consideration like that to stop you!'

'If you don't stop laughing at me, you're——' She was silenced as he jerked her back down on top of him and claimed her mouth hungrily again.

'Oh, yes...' she moaned several minutes later, the previous conversation having vanished from her mind. 'Thank God the alligator didn't get me,' she murmured, with heartfelt gratitude that she had been spared for a future of such unsurpassed ecstasy.

'Clearly he wasn't half as sneaky and conniving as me...' Rafael drawled, with rich self-satisfaction.

UNLOCK THE DOOR TO GREAT ROMANCE
AT BRIDE'S BAY RESORT

Join Harlequin's new across-the-lines series, set
in an exclusive hotel on an island off the coast of
South Carolina.

Seven of your favorite authors will bring you exciting stories
about fascinating heroes and heroines discovering love at
Bride's Bay Resort.

Look for these fabulous stories coming to a store near you
beginning in January 1996.

Harlequin American Romance #613 in January
Matchmaking Baby by Cathy Gillen Thacker

Harlequin Presents #1794 in February
Indiscretions by Robyn Donald

Harlequin Intrigue #362 in March
Love and Lies by Dawn Stewardson

Harlequin Romance #3404 in April
Make Believe Engagement by Day Leclaire

Harlequin Temptation #588 in May
Stranger in the Night by Roseanne Williams

Harlequin Superromance #695 in June
Married to a Stranger by Connie Bennett

Harlequin Historicals #324 in July
Dulcie's Gift by Ruth Langan

Visit Bride's Bay Resort each month wherever
Harlequin books are sold.

HARLEQUIN  PRESENTS®

Don't be late for the wedding!

Be sure to make a date in your diary for the happy event—
the latest in our tantalizing new selection of stories...

Wedlocked!

Bonded in matrimony, torn by desire...

Coming next month:

THE ULTIMATE BETRAYAL by Michelle Reid
Harlequin Presents #1799

"...an explosive magic that only (Michelle) Reid can create."
—*Affaire de Coeur*

The perfect marriage...the perfect family? That's what
Rachel Masterton had always believed she and her husband
Daniel shared. Then Rachel was told that Daniel had betrayed
her and she realized that she had to fight to save her marriage.
But she also had to fight to forgive Daniel for this...the
ultimate betrayal.

Available in March wherever Harlequin books are sold.